EAR

To

EAR

TIM NEUN

Publishing Partners

Publishing Partners
Port Townsend, WA
books@publishing-partners.com
www.MarciaBreece.com

Library of Congress Control Number : 2020918570
ISBN: 978-1-944887-63-6
ebook ISBN: 978-1-944887-64-3

Book design: Tim Neun
Cover design: Tim Neun
Editing: Cindy Hunter
Production: Marcia Breece

Table of Contents

Acknowledgments vii

Cindy's Foreword ix

Cindy's Honest Foreword...................................xi

Mike's Foreword.. xiii

Preface...xv

Dedication...xix

Introduction...xxi

Cast of characters.. xxiii

1. Prison? 1

2. Whitey blues 3

3. Kid, you are screwed.......................................5

4. Pee talk...9

5. Zeke, your wheelchair is shit.........................13

6. Left in the dust..21

7. Hi Mmurphlerg!..37

8. We're all going to die!.................................... 41

9. My allure vanishes 53

10. Zeke nearly gets creamed...........................57

11. The title of this chapter is longer than
    my high school football career....................... 61

12. How I save Lucy and fuck myself 69

13. 300+ empties in the back seat 81

14. 1st hangover, Sony & Cher, squawking
I Got You Babe, at 5:30 am 117

15. I miss my opportunity to kill Marv,
Dang 131

16. Sliced and diced by a baby cougar 135

17. I miss my 2nd chance to kill Mar 141

18. A claustrophobic elevator ride to
olfactory hell while blazing on LSD 145

19. Dr. Midnite to the rescue 151

20. The dull green room 165

21. My life of crime comes to an end 171

22. Prison, a highpoint in my life 175

23. Probation hell in Sun Valley 191

24. Torment 195

25. Epilogue 197

About the Author 199

Glossary 201

Discussion guide 213

Acknowledgments

'd like to thank two people who supported my efforts and gave me encouragement from the very beginning of this project.

My lovely, Sweet Double Happiness, (thank Lord Buckly) wife, Cindy Hunter, and my brother, Mike Neun. Both read the 1st draft and liked it! "This is good!" They said with genuine surprise. Telling 'eh?

Cindy became my editor and proofreader for a number of good reasons. She's here with me, she knows punctuation (I can't spell punkunation), I didn't have to pay her, (trust me, I paid dearly) and, most importantly, she likes to laugh.

The ski bum part of me could care less about commas, quotation marks, plot, character development, all that writing stuff. Both Cindy and Mike convinced me these qualities might be appreciated in a book.

Tragically, editing my book was not at the top of Cindy's to do list. Gardening, her new chickens, (I'm developing a new BBQ sauce specifically for these chickens) cleaning and laundry took precedence. I know, I couldn't believe it either.

You may also find it hard to believe, as it was for me, but standing over her shoulder while she was gardening, cleaning, doing the laundry, and tapping my foot nervously and loudly (which is tough in flip flops), only slowed her editing duties down.

I hear you, "Well Tim, why didn't you help with the cleaning and the laundry?"

Hey, lighten up, I do my part, plus I was busy rewriting all her damn edits!

She also grew weary of me falling dramatically to the floor, kicking and flailing my arms and doing that fake sobbing thing, like a seventy one year old, knowing edit number thirty five needed to be done. Had I known the editing would be hell on earth I never would have started this book!

Cindy was also responsible for many of the images. The good ones. I can't thank her enough.

Mike Neun, my far older brother, also liked the first draft and saw potential. Without his incessant badgering and encouragement I would have quit prior to page four. He was pissed because he thought it was better than the book he was working on and he is a real writer! Talk about incentive!

Cindy's Foreword

Tim is an artist. With wood and clay. We know Tim can write because everyone looks forward to his epoch e-mails. But a book? He never mentioned writing a book.

He sounded serious about this book and within a few days he presented me with a few pages of an incredibly good story. Of course it had no punctuation or sentence structure and so I naturally began to edit the thing. Shockingly, he seemed to appreciate my efforts.

We had been searching for a way to be creative together. He could not get into gardening and I gave his paintings less than average reviews. When the book came along and we reviewed and discussed the characters, their stories, and Tim's wild creation, I knew we had found our project. Then he decided he needed illustrations! He wanted me to help with the illustrations! Luckily, we both have mediocre standards and so we were satisfied with lackluster work. That made it more fun.

The book has had Tim up before dawn and working hour after hour writing, rewriting, drawing, painting, and learning all about Kerning (see glossary). Some days I consider contacting Tabitha King (not just Steven King's wife) to see if she had any tips on how to handle a creative genius in the throes of a project.

Tim is a dedicated author with a brilliant first book. It is nothing like any book you have ever read. You are going to love this book as much as I do. I am Cindy Hunter, Tim's wife and editor.

Cindy's Honest Foreword

I am Cindy Hunter (not just Tim's wife). This should have been my book. I always wanted to be a writer. Some of my education is in English literature and education so I know about the mechanics of writing. Tim is innocent of the knowledge of sentence structure, grammar, and punctuation.

I have had adventures, too. You would not believe how many interesting things I have done. I have lots of great ideas. Believe me, I could write a great book. It is simply crazy that this is not MY book. I cannot believe it.

The thing is, as astonishing as it is, Tim was the one who put pen to paper.

Bummer, jerk. Oh well, at least I am his wife AND EDITOR!

Mike Neun's Foreword

I first met the author, Tim Neun, when Mom and Dad brought him home from the hospital. Nancy (our sister) and I thought he was cute. Little did we know that just seventy-one years later he would sit down and write a book with himself as the main character and us in the tiniest of bit parts. Some siblings would be quite angry about that, and you can include us in that number.

Also, in all those years we never realized we were living with a cold-blooded killer, so it's possible we weren't paying attention. Hey, we had our own lives to lead and our own victims to murder, but why dwell on that now? Family. It's all about family.

This book is a tour de force (tour de France?) (I get those mixed up) in the mystery field, totally different from anything you've ever read. Seriously, I am a mystery addict and I have never come across a plot like this, or an ending this bizarre. I'm astounded my brother--the ski bum, artist, furniture maker, writer of the world's funniest e-mails—came up with this and it's a shame he didn't find his true calling as a novelist years ago.

On top of that, this book is illustrated! Personally! With drawings that could've been done by Rembrandt in his early years (maybe age two or three). You will giggle. I guarantee it.

I have written three books and I can honestly say I enjoyed *Ear to Ear* more. This pisses me off and I have written him out of my will.

Here is his book. It's good. Too good if you ask me.

Mike Neun, brother.

Preface

The idea of writing this story grew around my decision to refuse induction into the United States Armed Forces.

Back in 1970 I had concluded that war, in general, was an astonishingly stupid idea. It only seemed to make money for the armament manufacturers. My reason for refusing induction was not based on moral convictions. I did not consider myself a conscientious objector. By then I knew I was an atheist. The religious reasons used to avoid Vietnam were not available to me. I simply did not believe a single word spewing from our leaders. I wasn't about to kill or be killed for their blatant, bullshit lies. Looking back, it is sad to realize they were rank amateur lairs compared to our current shit-for-brains #45 president.

I wrote what I hope is a humorous tale. I glanced off all the serious quandaries, murder, rape, more murders, leaving them in your moral lap.

It was easy writing a book except for the writing part. Editing? Editing is hell on earth! I spent more time editing the fucking thing than writing it. Big time authors hire professional editors. They value their sanity!

To make matters worse I had an old copy of InDesign (CS6) (released in 1839) so I decided to format it myself. How difficult could learning a complex (for me) Adobe computer program be? I'm still not done and it has been two months of sitting in front of the (old-slow, low memory) computer for ten or twelve hours a day. But I reasoned trying to learn it would be a good project during this pandemic. More importantly what the fuck else have I got to do? Work on the house? Clean, paint, rebuild the deck then power wash it and re-stain it. Cindy just reminded me of the blistering exterior paint that needs scraping, sanding, priming and repainting just so it can blister again. Yeah, right.

After getting into the formatting I learned to appreciate typology. Before March of 2020, I didn't know typology existed. Good typology has changed how I read a book, for the better. Now I notice the art of drop caps, kerning, leading, the lack of orphans and much more.

Deciding to include images in a fictional novel arose from being told it hasn't been done before. Then I can be the first! Are you sensing a theme here? I started working on them, then quickly remembered, I can't draw. Then I began whining incessantly and conned Cindy into doing much of the work on them. The good ones are hers. Sadly, mine stand out for the wrong reasons.

You should know all this droning on verbiage is included to bulk up the word and page counts. *Ear to Ear* was not much more than a pamphlet. Kind of short. Instead of writing and editing more and risking my current "stable genius" status, I decided to take the road easily traveled and bulk it up with random stuff. Images, page count. A glossary in fiction? Word count. Discussion guide, word count.

I'm hoping to use high quality paper to make the this book thicker. I used margins wide enough to turn around a log truck. I worked in the woods blowing up stumps and rock one summer. You would be amazed how little room the drivers need to turn a giant log truck around. So, huge margins? You guessed it, page count.

These extra wide margins also allow room for you to take notes, with a giant sharpie. I'm assuming Ear to Ear will become a text book which will then sell for $150.00. At that point I will flip my outrage about the student debt situation completely around. Get a bigger loan, buy my book! Buy a bunch of them. *Ear to Ear* would make a wonderful gift for all your friends especially if you want to ditch a few of them.

Dedication

Ear to Ear is dedicated to three great guys who loved to laugh, blow shit up and taught me to ski.

Leo Scheiblehner
Dieter Oberbichler
Adi Weissensteiner

Leo & Tim at Mt. Bachelor

Introduction

As the hardest working character in this book, I thought my task was complete. The time to publish this thing was drawing near and Tim didn't have the foggiest idea of how to write an introduction without giving the entire plot (which is quite thin) completely away.

Tim asked if I would write it. I agreed, but pointed out a substantial pay raise was required per my contract. I negotiated both a nice bonus and an added scene that featured me in a favorable light.

Ear to Ear is a quasi-fictitious novel that includes images. Images are highly unusual in a novel. It's just not done. Authors take pride in describing scenes with words that convey to the reader a vivid picture. They paint with the eloquent, skillful use of words. Trust me, the images are immensely helpful per Tim's word-smith talent.

My lovely breasts are written about in depth, fortunately there is no drawing. It would have been horrific due to his profound lack of artistic talent. Too bad he didn't ask Cindy to draw them. She has talent and the drawing would have been bitchin'.

Not a bad intro 'eh. Filled up a page with random verbiage and you haven't a clue what's coming up. Where's my bonus?

Enjoy my new scene,
Lucy

Cast of characters in order of appearance.

Cast of characters in order of appearance.

Demi	Patrick Swazye	Delbert Hydros
Evelyn Hydros	Jack Neun	Mob Boss
Mobster	Mobster 2	Mobster
Jane Mansfield	Mike Neun	Nancy Neun
Lucy's Dad	Cop	Rob

Cast of characters in order of appearance.

Joshua Prouty	Doyle	Karl
Darleen	Fawn	Eileen
Dave Gast	Marv	Brenda
Bob Merriwether	Murf	Sea Lion
Cindy	Leo	Judy

Tim Neun

Cast of characters in order of appearance.

Kathy

Hurly

Biff

Buffy

Army Guy

Cletus

Earl

Lawyer

Judge

ChoMo

Walkin Death

Booger

Larry Long

Mumbles

Spaz

Cast of characters in order of appearance.

| Thumbs | Brian | Mark Ackerman |
| Vi | Lloyd | Zeke's Stunt Double |

. FEB   64

Jack & Kay Neun in Sun Valley

Tim Neun

Lefty Bowl in Sun Valley

CHAPTER 1

Prison?

My first night in prison I was raped by a couple of sadistic pedophiles. That was a Friday night. By Wednesday morning they were both dead.

What the fuck was I doing in prison?

FEDERAL INMATE #4926-N-666

Chapter 2

Whitey Blues

Let's sing a lighthearted tune written by a privileged white guy.

I was born in a shack
Way down on the tracks
All around us were tramps
We smoked all their crack
Which would have been tough
'Cause it taint' been 'vented yet
Then our mom done decided
To cook up some meth
She faked the recipe
Her equipment was sub-par
She blew up the tracks
Along with our shack
We just moved to Grosse Ille
'Cause our dad was real sharp
And made lots of scratch
We lived high on the hog
& owned huge Cadillacs
That floated over the tracks
Privileged white kids
Singin' whitey blues
In the back

CHAPTER 3

Kid, You are Screwed

H igh school was an eye opener for me. It was a four-year school so all of a sudden my freshman classmates and I were the newbies. I learned this immediately on walking through the front door my first day. *Newbies* is a highly derogatory term usually prefaced with the word *fuckin'*.

The girls, many of whom had rocketed through puberty over the summer, were now prancing around with their new perky breasts thrust under the noses of the older, in the know, guys. Little did they know that many of those protruding glands contained more tissue paper than, well, glands. A few reveled in their new found maturity. Apparently a very few reveled more enthusiastically. Within days those select few became *popular* in a way I did not fathom.

We were given the opportunity to take two electives along with the usual mind-numbing crap. My councilor, Mr. Stone, reviewed my junior high records. His demeanor changed from, "Welcome to freshman year!" to, "This poor kid is screwed." Then he made two suggestions which turned out to be life changing.

"First, you are going to take ceramics."

"Ceramics? What the hell is ceramics?" A couple of years earlier I had dropped some heirloom teacup of my mom's and the shit hit the fan. "I'm grounded for a WEEK for breaking a teacup? Jeeze Mom, just buy a new one!" At which point all hell broke loose and I was grounded for another week. That was the extent of my ceramics knowledge. "Cool, I'll just make my mom another heirloom teacup, it can't be that tough."

Mr. Stones other *suggestion* was that I would, later that day, start tutoring the physically and mentally disabled kids. "The Tards?" Hey, it was 1964 and sadly that word and many others had yet to be deemed not only offensive but racist, bigoted and, when used in the company of the wrong person, a sure way to get beat up. Mr. Stone was way ahead of that curve and took a few moments to straighten me out then and there. I'm proud to say that after spending some time with *The Tards* I understood how that word, coming from me, made them feel and I never used it again. The part I didn't get was they called each other *Tards* all the fucking time but I couldn't. Weird, eh!

At the appointed time I peeked into what was widely referred to as *the Crip room*. I was still confused. Somehow *Crip* was OK but *Tard* was not? The scene in the room was absolute mayhem. The noise was deafening and there was no apparent order. Mr. Stone, their teacher, waved me in, smiling, while any kid who could, greeted me by flipping me the bird, as best they could. In a mocking sing song cacophony they blurted out, "Tutor, tutor, tutor, hey Mr. know-it-all tutor." Mr. Stone turned to me, shrugged his shoulders, then turned back to the kids and sternly told them to shut up and in unison they told him to piss off and laughed even louder. "Don't worry," Mr. Stone said chuckling, "in this room that's how it works."

I was taken aback and highly intrigued by the overall lack of respect. Everybody was giving each other a boatload of shit and laughing loudly about it. I got behind this and immediately felt at home. I turned to the kids, held up both arms and waving them wildly, flipped them the bird and said, "You bunch of punks, go fuck yourselves!" They went wild with smiles and laughter. I was in.

Over time, I helped a very few of them when they had difficulties with some subject. We quickly concluded that me tutoring them was a joke as they were all far smarter than me. Mostly they tutored me. I might not have graduated without their help.

They were nice kids who fully realized they had been dealt a unique, difficult hand in life. We talked about, "Why me?" quite a bit.

Some swore like sailors. Many of the girls were astoundingly foul mouthed, which was refreshing. They constantly gave each other shit about their fucked up predicaments. We laughed a lot. I grew to like them and ended up feeling a stronger bond to them than most of the other kids in school.

CHAPTER 4

Pee Talk

The only previous experience I'd had with disabled kids was when we lived in Bellevue, Washington, a suburb of Seattle. I was eight or nine years old and my best friend, Paul, lived with his family next door. His younger sister, Mary, was six and had cerebral palsy so she was always strapped into her wheelchair. She flopped around a lot. It was really tough for me to understand her speech. Paul had two older brothers and we all hung out at their house most of the time. Mary always hung around with us playing games inside or we rolled her around outside when it wasn't raining.

PAUL

Paul and his brothers knew exactly what Mary was saying and translated for me. In a short time and with her brothers' help, I was able to understand her and realized she was quite a character. In my eyes her disability vanished even though she was strapped to a wheelchair. I didn't see Mary as disabled. I just saw Mary. It was weird.

She was a jokester and loved to laugh more than anything else. Her brothers pranked her relentlessly and she loved it. They loved her and she knew it. We spent hours devising pranks she could pull on *the boys*. She especially liked to be pushed by one of us while the rest of us chased after her yelling, "We're gonna get you and tickle you." Then the *pusher* would turn her around and she would chase us screaming, "I'm gonna get you and tickle you!" The whole point being she would eventually bash into one of us and then that person would make a big production of falling onto her then rolling off and collapsing on the floor. We had to fake a major injury while rolling around on the floor pretending to cry and sob while grabbing the afflicted leg, arm, or head. "Oh Mary, you bashed into Paul and he's going to die!" She would crack up and the smile on her face and the joy in her eyes expressed pure happiness.

She also loved to play hide and seek outside. One of us would move her to, well it just didn't matter where, right out in the open was fine. Then we would wander around calling her name. "Mary, oh Mary, we're gonna find you then jump out and scare you and tickle you until you pee your pants." She thought *pee* talk was the funniest thing ever, even more than we did! We made a point of passing right in front of her over and over while calling her name and pretending we could not find her. She got pretty animated yelling at us, "I'm here, right here." Then we would turn and jump up and down and act like she scared the shit out of us. It drove her wild with laughter. She had a great laugh and she laughed a lot. She loved being one of the guys.

Their mom, Shirley, was Mother Teresa minus the religious crap. That summer, Shirley bought a brand new gigantic Mercury *woody* station wagon. Then she announced she was taking us all to Disneyland! Talk about peeing my pants!

We were quite the traveling troupe. Shirley, four young boys and Mary flopping around in her wheelchair. We caused quite a stir wherever we went.

In 1957 there were no accommodations for disabled kids or adults anywhere, including Disneyland. At each ride we had to lift Mary out of her wheelchair and carry her up to the ride. There were no ramps. Then we strapped

OFF TO DISNEYLAND!

Tim Neun

her into the ride with our own straps. The seat belts on the rides? They were worthless for Mary's small, out-of-control body, so we didn't trust them or use them. One of us always rode with her, trying our best to keep her from flying out. We also had to hold her head steady. She had the habit of throwing her bony arms wildly in the air when she was excited and she was excited from the moment she got into the ride until we unstrapped her and lifted her out. She did this on every single ride, even the lame-ass Teacup. Her elbows were sharp and the term *loose cannon* described her movements perfectly. All of us ended up with painful, nasty bruises on our faces, arms and chests. By the time we departed Disneyland we all looked like we had been in a gang rumble and had barely escaped with our lives. Mary laughed at our sorry, beat-to-shit bodies and never tired of bragging about how she beat the crap out of us. She was very proud of herself.

We took Mary on every single ride at Disneyland. We could count on her to scream bloody murder at the top of her lungs pretending to be scared, but her laughter gave her away. She loved every minute of that trip just as much as I did.

We drove back to Seattle exhausted and happy. Within a couple of weeks my family moved to Portland, Oregon. I never saw Mary or her brothers again.

CHAPTER 5

Zeke, Your Wheelchair is Shit

Mary was my only experience with disabled kids prior to being thrust into *cripworld*. Now I'm surrounded by twenty two of the little ingrates for an hour every other day. Little did I know these same kids would provide more joy to my life than I could ever imagine.

The radio was always on in the crip room. More and more the news carried stories of war. Someplace called Vietnam. Mr. Stone talked about this war in Southeast Asia and pulled down the map and showed us where it was, just south of China.

He said the Chinese were Communists and explained how communism differed from democracy. On the surface communism sounded good but even at fourteen we had our doubts. Apparently, the commies were using Laos and Cambodia to sneak into Vietnam to take it over. The recent history of that part of the world was a mess. We talked about Vietnam quite a bit. We studied about how the screwed up history of the area led to its screwed up present.

Joan was one of the *crips*. She was a loner and usually sat at the back of the class. Her legs didn't work well for reasons she never revealed to me. She used the *Lofstrand* style crutches (named after the inventor) with the aluminum half circles that gripped her forearms.

Over the next few weeks I got to know her a little bit. She was blindingly smart and had a wicked sense of humor. She was also a math wiz and she ended up tutoring me in algebra.

LOFTSTRAND CRUTCH

The bullies, outside of the *criproom*, hassled these kids relentlessly. They called them names and made a point of making their journey in school even more difficult. One of them, Byron Hydros, seemed to really have it in for Joan. At six feet tall she looked like a model who lifted weights. She did. Her folks owned a boxing club in Portland and she worked out all the time. She was pretty imposing and maybe that's what drove Hydros crazy enough to bug her. She was taller than he was, smarter than him, and she had a vicious sense of humor. All traits he profoundly lacked.

Whenever I saw Hydros mocking her, she ripped him to shreds. He was a typical bully; he kept his backup buddies close, but they had no loyalty. When she tore him a new one, they cracked up. Oddly, he never caught on. He wasn't that sharp, a fact well known around school. He must have gotten some bizarre thrill out of being put down by her and laughed at by his pals. It drove him crazy and sometimes it threw him into a blind rage. He kicked the lockers hard enough to put dents in them. He broke his big toe once. A couple of times he drew his fist back like he was going to hit her. I think she wanted him to; Joan knew her boxing skills were superior and she knew how to use her crutches as weapons. She was just waiting for a chance to pummel his sorry ass into the ground. Something was going on there that I didn't understand.

Zeke was another one of the kids I got to know pretty well. What a great name, eh? I told him, "Your wheelchair is a genuine piece of shit." He nodded his head in agreement. It didn't fit him. It was tough to steer and it barely rolled. His family was not that well off so it was the best they could come up with. I knew there were auto and machine shop classes at school. They were located in a big building just across the main parking lot. Zeke and I headed over to check them out. I immediately learned the difficulty people in wheelchairs face just getting from point A to point B. There must have been eight curbs to tackle and a slope with a set of steep stairs where I almost lost him. "Jeeze, Zeke, it would have been good to know the brake doesn't work!" He laughed, "I took the brake off!"

We rolled into the main building and when he saw all the welders, grinders, machine tools (which included two lathes and a huge Bridgeport knee mill), Zeke's eyes lit up, "This is my kind of joint!" The kids in the class greeted us with jubilant cheers of welcome, NOT. Blank stares mostly.

Some old guy, he must have been almost thirty-five, turned out to be the shop teacher, Mr. Barber. He strolled over and asked what buildings we were looking for. "These buildings right here, the auto and machine shops." He was perplexed. "What could these kids want here?"

Zeke spoke up, "My wheel chair is a piece of crap and I've got some ideas on how to improve it."

BRIDGEPORT KNEE MILL

EAR TO EAR

Mr. Barber and the students turned to me as they had no clue what Zeke had just said per his difficulty with speech. I translated: "Zeke said his chair is a total piece of shit, as you can plainly see. He has some specific ideas about what and how it could be fixed and made more user friendly." That piqued their interest and they drew in a little closer.

Zeke and I could sense the gears in their heads beginning to churn. A wheelchair? In auto shop? Mr. Barber was less than enthused. The students were more intrigued. Mr. Barber picked up on this and grudgingly said, "Ok we will give you a hand fixing up your wheelchair. It is easy to see it really is a piece of shit and I think we can help you out.

Zeke turned to me and smiling broadly whispered, "Watch this."

Zeke pointed out everything wrong with his chair and exactly how he wanted it fixed and the improvements to make, all of which he had designed in his head. Slowly it dawned on all of us that his ideas were brilliant. Mr. Barber was impressed and asked Zeke if he had any other interesting projects he was working on. It turns out Zeke was a mechanical design genius.

After hearing just two of Zeke's new ideas: A radically different type of

ZEKE'S OLD CHAIR

sewage treatment plant and a paving material that was self healing. Mr. Barber slowly turned to his students. Their mouths hung wide open, eyebrows were raised and eyes were popping out.

Mr. Barber said, "You guys are lucky I don't grade on the curve, eh!" They all nodded their heads in agreement. They were outclassed and knew it. At that moment they knew Zeke, this kid in a wheelchair who could barely talk, was a brainiac.

Zeke had a completely new design fully developed in his head for a prototype wheelchair that utilized four wheel drive, a rechargeable six volt battery motor, and a sophisticated hydraulic suspension system that allowed the chair to go over curbs and negotiate stairs with

ZEKE'S 1ST PROTOTYPE

ease. It was controlled by brain waves that gave the severely disabled person complete control over every possible movement of the vehicle. Mechanically it was brilliant and his electronics were thirty years ahead of his time.

Mr. Barber and the students were stunned. They smiled and nodded their heads in agreement. "Yeah, we can do this," he said. "It will take the whole year but this is a great project!"

After that day Zeke spent most of his time in the shop designing and helping to make his chair. By his junior year his new chair was built and working. It needed some tweaks so the second prototype was being worked on in the shop. After that chair was completed, it won numerous design competitions held throughout eleven western states. Zeke was as big a hero as the school's athletes. While in his senior year Zeke developed the financial backing to invest in his wheelchair design. He started a sophisticated machine shop to make all the parts as well as an assembly plant in the adjoining complex. Zeke's assembly plant utilized robotics to remove humans from dangerous procedures and an overhead system that delivered the correct part to the proper station at exactly the right moment. Zeke was a design genius and savvy businessman, a combo rarely seen. By the time he was twenty-five he had become a multimillionaire.

Mr. Barber was named teacher of the year in 1966. He recognized Zeke's genius and became his mentor. Zeke also pushed Mr. Barber to recruit girls into the auto and machine shop programs. "Chicks, where's the chicks? There's no chicks in these shops! We demand chicks!" Zeke was obviously ahead of his time design wise but his social awareness was deeply rooted in the 1930's.

The first girls came from the *criproom* as Zeke knew them and knew they had some great ideas. They flourished. Within two years fifty percent of the students in all the shop classes were females. That inclusion and realization that girls were just as capable as any guy in the shops probably had more to do with the teacher of the year award than Zeke's individual success. It was a step, but as we all know, that struggle continues today.

Twenty years later, Steven Hawking asked Zeke to design a new chair for him based on the original. Zeke told him that was a really stupid idea and came up with a radically new design specifically for him. Hawking cracked up about being told he was stupid, but he and Zeke formed a close friendship that lasted all of Steven's life. Zeke was also instrumental with the formation and implementation of the ADA act.

I have stayed in touch with Zeke over the years and he is doing great. He is the same funny, brilliant and humble guy. He has been in a wheelchair all his life and he feels fortunate. Zeke has never uttered a word about the car wreck. He is a man of unblemished honor.

CHAPTER 6

Left in the dust

Back at *cripworld*, I learned Mr. Stone usually ended each class with a makeshift music appreciation segment. We listened to everything. Classical, jazz, rock and roll, anything and everything. We brought records from home, each of us trying to come up with music no one else had ever heard. Everyone tried to outdo the other with the most unusual or original music.

One day this kid brought in a new album his parents had given him. They were old beatniks who transitioned into hippies and smoked pot, whatever that was. They sounded weird. So Mr. Stone put the record on the turntable with a grin, he had just heard it and knew what was coming. He made of point of cranking up the volume. We listened to the whole album. When it was over no one could move. We looked at each other with our eyes and mouths open wide. Completely blown away. Jimi Hendrix. It was quite an experience and it took our music appreciation to a whole new level.

I'd been bringing in stuff my parents had, Perry Como, Frank Sinatra, Dean Martin.

From that geezer shit of my parents to Hendrix was not only a sudden but a giant leap. Jimi was ours. He was young, we were young and his music and lyrics spoke to us. Not to our parents, only and directly to us. Our parents didn't get it. Teens throughout history have made a distinct move to distant themselves from their parents. It catches the parents like a deer in the headlights. They have no clue how it happens but they know something big is going on and they are not part of it. They are left in the dust. I am now a parent and grandfather and know that feeling of being left behind. It comes as a shock, it's heartbreaking, but necessary.

Another kid brought in a record by a guy named Thelonious Monk, some old, black, jazz dude. My knowledge of jazz was zippo, but

THELONIUS MONK

I really liked this guy's style. I liked the slow pace. The notes not played. Monk still surprises and moves me and he is one of my all-time favorites.

Another great thing happened that freshman year. I got to tag along with a couple of older guys to a concert at Lewis and Clark College. I had no idea who was playing but it was cheap, the guys were willing to take me, and there would be college girls. They talked about meeting college girls; I just wanted to see what a college girl looked like. Turns out they looked great.

The curtain rose and for the next two and a half hours the entire audience stood in amazement and wonder. Nothing in life had prepared me for this.

Frank Zappa and the Mothers of Invention. Nothing in life would have prepared anybody for Frank Zappa and the Mothers. His music changed my life. It was loud. It was sarcastic. It was complicated. In Frank's own words it was *Bizarre*. It certainly wasn't the normal Beach Boys or Bee Gees bubblegum bullshit played on the local radio station.

I bought the album the next day and listened to it over and over all weekend. My parents, in Frank's own words, yelled into my room, "TURN IT DOWN, TURN IT DOWN!" I played the record in our class on Monday and the kids went wild. Even Mr. Stone liked it. Two days later the kids put on a short concert for Mr. Stone and me.

FRANK ZAPPA

Put yourself in our shoes as the kids, visibly excited, arranged themselves in the front of the room and ordered us to sit in the back and keep our mouths shut and listen, to what, we hadn't a clue.

Then, with no background music, a cappella, they cranked out "Concentration Moon" from the *Mothers* album. From high notes to low, the change ups, everything, they sang it perfectly. Unbeknownst to Mr. Stone and me a number of the kids had powerful and beautiful voices and their arrangement was dead on. They superbly communicated the humor and pathos of the song and of Frank Zappa. They integrated the verbalizations of kids with speech impediments and those voices that were wildly out of key. They used them to perfectly convey the sarcasm so prevalent in Frank's music.

The term *disabled* kept fading further away from my perception and I was beginning to understand I had disabilities but a body that worked. It kept my mental ones well hidden. None of us are perfect; we all have disabilities in one form or another. Some people are decidedly unaware of theirs, and that is truly a debilitating disability!

CHAPTER 7

Hi Mmurmphleg!

My next elective was ceramics which turned out to be another life changer. Don't get all enthused; initially it was a fucking nightmare.

I walked in about five minutes late the first day and was greeted by twenty-three pairs of eyes, all girls, staring at me in disbelief. "A guy in ceramics?" "Loser." No other guys, not one. Sure the teacher, Mr. Thornton was a guy, but he didn't count. Fuck me runnin'. I may as well have been in the home economics class wearing an apron, baking shit and sewing it together.

I knew the crap soon to be received from my friends would be severe and relentless the moment I walked out of ceramics class. "Hey Timmy," they loved calling me Timmy, (assholes) "can you make me a special ashtray in your girlie pottery class just for me? Do you have to wear an apron?" Oh well, how bad could it be? Worse than you can imagine.

Remember, twenty-three girls and me. I struggled when it came to talking to girls.

OK, struggle is a misrepresentation. More like mortification, coupled with terror, and praying-to-god some life threatening event like the commies dropped an A-bomb right where I was standing, or worse.

When a girl, any girl, maybe at the A&W, in ceramics class or in the hall at school, said, "Hi Tim," my internal mental sequencer would clunk into low gear. "Oh my god, she is looking right at me and her lips are moving." Every sound was magnified except for her voice. I'd go deaf. I wonder what she said? Was she really speaking to me? I'd start to sweat. No, that's not right; I didn't *start* to sweat. My body unleashed a torrent of fluid that gushed uncontrollably from every pore.

I would attempt a witty answer but my brain had switched from low gear to no gear. Brain off? Brain on? Brain definitely off. I began to twitch. "My legs! My legs are gone!" This all happened in unison, in less than a millisecond. I held my ground with my mouth wide open, drool dripping from each corner and my eyes glazed over. My mind screamed, "Run Tim, run for your life!"

Like a fool, I stood my ground. Hey, I'm a guy. Slowly I gained what little composure was left while my remaining self-respect, taunted me with, "You're a big time loser, girls freak you out, HaHaHaHaHaaaHa. See you in a year or four or maybe never!"

I looked directly into her beautiful blue eyes and brightly said, "Hi Mmurmphleg."

Fortunately my two second window of opportunity had slammed shut and she was already three feet past me. All she heard was "Hi Mmurphleg," which I gathered was not her name. Rack 'em up boys and cut another notch in the old belt!

Mr. Thornton led me to the back of the classroom and gestured to what I would soon learn was a potter's wheel. Yeah, so now what? It was the only wheel in the room and I was the only guy. Slowly it dawned on me that I was to figure it out while the rest of the class, twenty three girls, would be using the rolling pins to make slab doodads.

Mr. Thornton took his time to demonstrate very clearly to the girls how to use

POTTER'S WHEEL

Tim Neun

the rolling pin to make flat slabs of clay which could then be made into all sorts of things. They worked feverishly and within minutes produced perfect slabs of clay. They helped each other devise methods to add interesting textures then cut the slabs up and joined them to make all sorts of plates, cups, containers and some art looking stuff. They were working together. They were helping each other. They were collaborating like it was some natural behavior.

Guys don't collaborate, we compete. Put twenty three guys together with rolling pins and two hundred pounds of clay and we would have sharpened the rolling pins into knives or fashioned them into clubs. The clay would be formed into fist sized balls, perfect for throwing. To be tossed through windows, stuck to the ceiling and smeared all over the floor. Did you know you can roll clay between your hands into six inch tapered rope shapes then jam them into your nose? They look like giant boogers! Twenty-three guys would discover this at the exact same moment. One minute there would be twenty-three guys sitting there with no clue, the next minute you would have twenty-three guys with giant clay boogers hanging from every nostril. That's forty five (Should have been forty six but the booger in Earl's left nostril kept falling out) well shaped boogers and not a single girl, not even one would figure that one out. And women think they are equal to men! Ha!

Just think of the possibilities if we could join forces: the collaborative talents of women and the creative side of men. We could have made enough clay boogers for the entire school in no time!

Mr. Thornton casually worked his way back to me and demonstrated how to *wedge the clay*. He did not bother to explain why the clay needed to be wedged. I assumed he noticed the lack of muscles in my arms, which were not hard to miss, and wedging the clay was some sort of ceramics body building exercise.

Over time I discovered wedging the clay was supposed to work the air bubbles out and make the clay perfectly homogeneous.

This gave *throwing* a pot and *firing* the pot a slightly better chance of success. My wedging technique introduced air bubbles and made the clay distinctly less homogeneous resulting in uneven *pots* that were doomed to blow up in the *kiln*.

Meanwhile, back on the wheel, there was not much collaboration happening

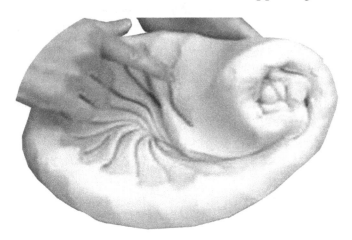

NICE CLAY WEDGING!

between my fingers and the clay. I'd slap the clay onto the wheel, slowly start it spinning, and without even touching it, watch it become more and more off center. Naturally my first reaction was to get pissed off, which led to my foot pressing down harder on the peddle, which increased the speed of the potter's wheel. In a heartbeat, it surpassed 8,000 RPM at which point I reached in to *center* the clay. The next moment I was sprawled on the floor looking up at the rapidly spinning ten pound chunk of clay. Exactly one nanosecond later I watched the clay fly off the wheel. In the next nanosecond I watched the clay, much like a meteor having traveled from the far side of the Milky Way Galaxy at just under the speed of light, slam directly into my groinal region. Even through the lightning bolts streaming from my eyes and over my loud gasps for air, I could sense twenty three girls feeling sorry for me, which did not drown out the cacophony of the Tee-Hee-Tee-Hees.

After physically recovering (mentally I've carried that emotional scar throughout my life), and getting back to the wheel, I managed to cover myself from head to toe with what looked to be brown runny shit. Mr. Thornton waltzed over and handed me, to my astonishment, *The Apron*. No, please dear God, not *The Apron*!

As if on cue, the twenty three girls swung around, now in matching, big time Broadway costumes, hands on their hips in perfect unison, pointing and wagging their fingers at me, they launched into a rousing version of, "Timmy's here and he's wearing a flowered apron," (sung to "My Boyfriend's Back") while performing an entire apron dance routine. It ended up that year's blockbuster musical "Apron Boy" which starred Jeffery, as me. My Gaydar, at that point in my life, was essentially non-existent, but even I noticed Jeffery in the halls. Christ, who hadn't. I was just learning the importance of tits. Gay stuff would take another couple of years for me to grasp. Jeffery was a brave pioneer.

Lucy was in my ceramics class. I didn't know her at all. She seemed nice but really quiet. Withdrawn. I knew she was on the lacrosse team and those girls were tough. Way tougher than me!

The other girls in the ceramics class were the stuck up popular girls, not Lucy. She openly disdained most of them. They were guarded and wisely kept their distance.

To be honest, Lucy was a bombshell. I say that as an astoundingly naive fourteen year old who didn't know what a bombshell was. She had piercing blue eyes. She was tall. She towered over my puny five foot five inch frame. Due to our difference in height, my view, when facing her and trying to talk, was her chest. It was a nice view.

I liked that view. I would instantly fall into a trance gazing at her boobs. She was well aware of that and would just place her left index finger under my chin and lift until my eyes met hers. Dang. I'll bet it got old for her. What she didn't seem to get tired of was giving me a gentle whack upside my head with her right hand at the same instant.

Her family occupied a top rung of wealth and status in the Northwest. She was humble and oddly quiet. Did she ski? That's what I cared about. Well, that and her lovely breasts were the extent of my interest. Even today, fifty three years later, I'm able, on a moment's notice, to conjure up a perfect mental image of her glands, anytime, anywhere.

Within a few days in ceramics class she drifted away from the rolling pin wielding slab builders and took up a spot at the wedging table next to the potter's wheel and me. Man, could she wedge clay! Her arms were twice the size of mine and she was strong. She could take a fifteen pound hunk of clay and have it ready to go in no time. So she wedged while I threw.

I was quite proud of the stuff I was making. Two inch tall semi cylindrical blob shapes that had thick bottoms, thin tops, thin bottoms, thick tops. I coveted each one as a masterpiece that inevitably blew up in the kiln. During those days, I learned to fully understand the meaning of a new word: angst.

Over time, like the next day, Lucy suggested we trade off the wedging/throwing tasks occasionally. Actually she meant right then, so we switched, right then. Throwing was hard for me because I was usually staring at her wedging the clay. Oh baby, oh baby you can wedge my loins whenever you want. Vaguely I sensed I might like that. Too bad I didn't know what a loin was.

We talked a bit, lacrosse, skiing, making fun of the slabbers, hardly serious stuff.

About a month into school, Lucy walked into ceramics class with her arm in a cast. My first thought was, "Man, ceramics is gonna be tough with just one arm," my second thought was, "What happened?"

The arm cast didn't seem that out of the ordinary for the lacrosse girls as they were always wandering around with bandages, black eyes, wrists in a cast or some appendage wrapped up. Lucy had a reputation as one of the bruisers on the team. When she sported a black eye, she made a point of smiling and giving me the best evil eye ever. As I said, she was quiet but had a sly sense of humor. I liked that about her.

Before this goes any further you need to quash your dirty, filthy, suggestive images of Demi Moore (Lucy) and Patrick Swazye (me) gushing uncontrollably all over some innocent, formless chunk of plastic movie prop clay slowly revolving seductively on the sweat glistened potter's wheel. Wet and slippery, a supple, flesh like clay, actually a high fire porcelain blend that was a silky white and yielded, with a firm resistance, to our every touch. I was thinking, what glaze shall we eagerly and endlessly rub all over the pot with our entwined hands? "Tim, oh Tim," her yearning voice cooed. I snapped out of that when her voice changed to a sharp, highly frustrated tone, "Tim, TIM! Jezus Christ, where were you and what the fuck are you doing? Don't apply the glaze now; it will fuck up the firing qualities of the clay!"

Back to Lucy showing up with a broken arm. I assumed something happened at the lacrosse game, but I missed the mark big time. Later in the day, I asked a couple of the girls on the lacrosse team if she broke it at practice, but all I got were down turned eyes and a mumbled, "Don't know." Chicks.

Next class, I was wedging and Lucy was throwing a nice pot with just one hand and her elbow! I knew my stuff was getting better but here she was throwing a tall, thin pot with just her hand and elbow! Bitch. Then the pot started to go south on her and she was visibly upset.

I tried to comfort her, "Hey, relax, when your arm heals up your technique will improve." Then she quietly started to cry which seemed to me a tad dramatic, "Jezus Lucy, it's just a pot."

"It's not the pot; it's my arm."

"Well, shit for brains, you've got a broken arm and you're using it to throw a pot! You are putting pressure on the break; it's bound to hurt, duh! Actually, you should be more concerned if it DOSEN'T hurt!"

Through her tears she managed a gentle smile and said, "It's not that it hurts, which it does, it's how it got broken."

Astounded. "How it got broken? Come on Lucy, when a guy breaks some appendage it is a badge to show off, to everybody, everywhere, all the time! You always cover your cast with your coat like you're embarrassed by it.

"For us guys an injury usually means we did something really stupid and we're proud of it, like falling out of a tree or seeing who can do the longest wheelie on his bike or going head first down the kiddie slide at the playground or going way too fast off some cornice on the mountain and totally blowing the landing. You know, guy stuff we can laugh and brag about. Hell, a broken arm is way cool! You get your friends to write on your cast, in giant red letters, words like shit and ass so you can nonchalantly stroll around school knowing the teachers can't do a damn thing! Lucy this is an opportunity, your broken arm is a fucking godsend!"

My joking, lighthearted enthusiasm did nothing to brighten her spirits. Wow, this is odd. That usually works. More importantly, it's all I've got.

You should know, my profound lack of being able to pick up on anything a woman says, except the blindingly obvious, has remained stuck at a fifth grade level for well over fifty years!

"Yeah, it hurts but, I'll tell you later, OK?"

An ominous chill coursed through my veins. Years later I equated that moment to my body realizing, from that moment on, I would not fully understand much of what women would ever say to me.

I went deep, as never before and asked her, "Seriously, how did you break your arm? I really want to know." I really didn't want to know nor did I give a shit but we (guys) say crap like this to show sincerity and compassion, whatever that is.

I waited and waited and waited some more. I was beginning to lose my patience.

"Fuckin A, what is the big fucking deal," I thought.

She looked me in the eye and said, "It is a secret and if I tell you, you will have to promise to not say a word, to anybody, ever."

"Sure, no sweat."

She continued, "And if you do tell anybody I'll break both your puny fucking arms in a heartbeat and you know I can do it."

No shit, I knew it. But like the fool I am, I promised. "Hey, how bad can it be?"

With tears streaming down her face she told me, "Byron did it."

"Byron? By accident? I mean he's your boyfriend."

"No, it was not an accident; well it was kind of an accident."

"Kind of an accident? Like what did you do, fall off his motorcycle? Was he showing you how to tackle or you were showing him how to block in lacrosse?"

Fuck me. "Not an accident, kind of an accident? Jezus please tell me what the fuck happened as I'm not picking up on this vague, it is, it isn't, bullshit."

"No, we were having another big argument and he got really mad and pushed me down the staircase at his house."

I didn't get it. I'd never been that mad at anybody to push anybody, on purpose, down a staircase.

"You must have done something terrible to make him do that! What the fuck did you do?"

To say that I was clueless is an understatement. I'd never heard of physical abuse. I didn't know it was a thing. I could not envision hurting a girl on purpose. Finally, incredulously, I blurted out, "Did he do it on purpose?"

"Yes. He has hurt me before. He slaps me. He punches me in the face, he kicks me."

"So all the black eyes, the bruises, he did them, not lacrosse?"

"Not lacrosse, he caused them all."

I was dumbfounded. I knew Byron was a bully but this shit was way beyond being a bully. Even I knew that. And to hit a girl intentionally trying to hurt her? Repeatedly? WTF?

She held back her tears and looked me dead in the eye, "He hits me and he makes me have sex when I don't want to."

My legs started to give out and I sat down next to her. The potter's wheel was still slowly going round and round.

"You know him, he's a mean bully and worse. You've watched him hassle the handicapped kids. He only goes after those least able to fight back. Don't get me wrong, he has his good side. He can be caring and surprisingly thoughtful. I think down deep he is an OK guy. That's the side of him I first got to know. I fell in love with that guy. He is like a little kid in a football player's body. He can't control himself. He snaps at anything. One minute he's laughing and a moment later his eyes glaze over and he turns into a monster."

Fuckfuckfuckfuck was the depth of my thinking. I was stunned, in shock. I had no idea this kind of shit existed.

"I try to help him. He grew up with it. It's all he knows. His dad, coach Hydros, does the exact same stuff to Byron's mom, Evelyn. I've heard him screaming at her. I've seen him hit her and I've seen her bruises and black eyes. He doesn't let her out of the house. He gets more angry than Byron. Byron says he does weird sex things to his younger brother and sister and beats them nearly everyday. Byron is turning into his father. Evelyn has warned me over and over to get away; Byron will only hurt you, or worse. I don't know where to turn because Byron has said he will kill himself or me or both of us if I leave him."

"Jezus, you have to get away from him. You don't have to put up with his shit. Somebody other than me needs to be told about this, like the cops."

"You promised you wouldn't tell a soul about this!"

"You can't be serious, he could kill you! Do your parents know?"

"No, Byron is very good about putting his sweet, polite face on when he is around my parents. They are totally self-absorbed with the country club, their charity work, my dad's business and traveling around the world. They think the world of him and probably trust him more than me!"

CHAPTER 8

We're all going to die!

started driving with my folks in the car when I was thirteen. Mom and Dad taught me just about everything I would need to know to be safe and self-reliant. Right off the bat, Dad took me to a wrecking yard and we just wandered around checking out all the smashed up cars and speculating the cause and the occupant's condition after the crash. Pretty grisly day, but educational as hell. Head on, dead. Rollover, probably dead. Side impact, the major ones, dead. Rear ender, snapped neck and confined to a wheelchair, if lucky. The skull-sized windshield hole, tailgating and probably not wearing a seatbelt, dead. We talked about how all these wrecks might have happened and came to the conclusion that a momentary lapse of concentration was all it took. "As a driver you must remain totally focused and fully aware of everything going on around you all the time," warned my father.

On the way home he asked me to observe the other drivers on the road and notice what they were doing: looking down and screwing with the radio, lighting a cigarette, looking at the passenger while talking, singing. One bozo had a map opened up and laid out on the steering wheel and would only occasionally look up. I was surprised to see so many people doing damn near everything but driving. No wonder they crashed all the time. Going to need more wrecking yards.

Our family skied and we owned a cabin in Government Camp on Mt. Hood. Right after dinner we would go over to the big parking lot at the Multipor Ski Area and practice driving on snow. Mom, Dad and I practiced how to control a skid, how to drift around a corner, how to stop in a straight line as quickly as possible, how to start in second gear with traction and not spin the tires. It was fun. In

GOVERNMENT CAMP

the moment, it evened the playing field for us. We laughed at each other's mistakes. We'd all be screaming and laughing at the same time, "We're all going to die!" It was one of the few times in my life that I actually got to have fun with my parents. They had a good time too.

Activity wise, the backseat was never mentioned. That would have been an awkward conversation.

They let me drive, by myself, when I turned fourteen. I was the last kid and an unplanned accident which may have had something to do with them being pretty lax in the child protective realm. They were both driving at fourteen and figured, what the hell, if they did I could. I guess to them the difference between 1928 and 1964 was immaterial. The only thing they said was, "Don't do anything stupid," meaning, "Don't get pulled over by the cops or your driving days will abruptly end." My kind of parenting!

1955 CADDY

They were not about to let me drive one of their cars, which at the time were gigantic Cadillacs, so they bought me a well-used VW Beetle. Per the wrecking yard experience and remembering the number of seriously damaged VW Beetles and knowing most of the occupants were also probably, seriously dead, let's just say I kept my eyes on the road at all times, scared. Later I wondered if they had considered a Corvair just to get rid of me sooner.

My dad figured out he could buy two year old Cadillacs for the same price as a new, shitty, Chevrolet. My dad's car was a yellow 1955 Cadillac Coupe De Ville with a white top. It really was a nice car, huge and comfortable. To get to the gas tank one had to press a small reflector on the taillight which would then pop up revealing the gas cap. It was a pretty cool feature.

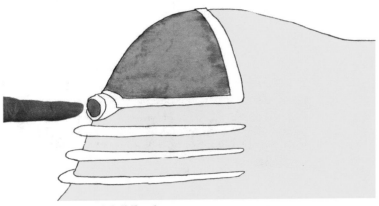

1955 CADDY GAS CAP

Most of the gas station attendants had never seen it. The attendants thought it was pretty cool when we showed them how it worked. All the windows were electric. The AC and heater were magnificent. The car always started and kept running. Most importantly, as an occupant, one possessed that special, "I'm better than you," Cadillac status. Apparently the status seeking luxury car buyer in 1955 did not consider *handling* an important feature. When *docking* at the country club, one's image was valued above all else. The owner of a Cadillac, back then, did not consider handling, stopping or acceleration as needed qualities in a car.

The allure of humongous Caddies, which are not usually valued for their snow country driving characteristics, waned for my dad after a couple of winters of putting on and taking off tire chains. He ended up buying a brand new Chevy Impala with a 396 cubic inch V-8, four on the floor with positraction. In the winter he mounted studded tires on it. That fucker was the penultimate snow car! He actually let me drive it! Oh yeah, it was also faster than shit, bright yellow and the definition of a chick magnet.

My mom's car was a 1959 Caddy. It had to have been one of the most massive sedans ever built, probably in a shipyard.

Everything about it was enormous. It had a gigantic V-8. It comfortably sat three adults in the front seat and four adults in the back and everybody was encased in baby soft calf leather. The trunk equaled the cubic area of a medium sized swimming pool. The mob utilized Cadillacs not only for the comfort, but the bullet stopping power of the all steel body and enormous trunk. Those black holes would comfortably hold three or four tied-up, hooded corpses, machine guns and ammo for the next four or five shoot outs.

Tail fins reached the pinnacle of size, engineered prowess, obscenity and popularity in 1959. These monsters were the eighth wonder of the world. They looked like something a stoned out Pharaoh dreamed up then sacrificed millions of slaves to build them. A pair of rocket shaped taillights were stylistically glommed on to each fin.

These fins came to a savage point behind the furthest protuberance of the car and were like daggers, sharp and dangerous in the untrained hand. Even more of a threat were the massive bumpers which were solid steel, accounting for nearly sixty percent of the entire weight of the car.

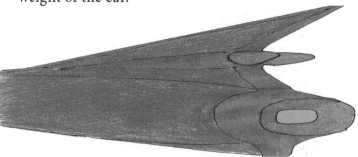

CADDY FINS THAT SLICE PAPER THIN SALAMI

drive. My mom made me drive it because she liked my VW bug. It was more her style and size. Tragically I was unable to take advantage of the Chevy's only redeeming feature, the ability to fold the back seat down and lure girls into it at the drive in theater. There was no luring. The car was not a chick magnet and with me driving it actually repelled girls.

* * *

Let me backtrack quite a bit. My brother, sister and I were born in Detroit, Michigan. If you picked up on that when you sang that catchy blues classic at the start of this book, you must be some kind of psychic, as Detroit was never mentioned. To me, Detroit may as well have been the moon because we lived on an idyllic island in the Detroit river, Grosse Ille. Compared to Detroit, it was like Tahiti but colder, flat as a pancake, and everybody was white, well off, and we didn't eat much mashed Taro root.

Dad worked for the Detroit Power Screwdriver Company. I had no clue what he or the company made. My guess was it had something to do with the auto industry. They turned screws, with power, in Detroit, wherever the hell that was.

He came home from work one day and announced we were moving to Seattle to start a new company named Hydraulic and Air Equipment Company. My brother, Mike and my sister, Nancy felt, well, I have no idea how they felt, nor did I give a shit. Lighten up; I was only eight years old! For all I knew Seattle was in Indiana or India. At this point in my life I was just a clueless passenger.

We loaded up the Caddys and headed west. The only thing I remember about the entire eight day drive from Detroit to Seattle was Mike and I working to prank our parents. I sat on Mike's lap while we drove past our parents. I steered while we passed Mom and Dad. Mike put both his arms out the driver's window and waved frantically at them. We were a sophisticated and safety conscious family. When my dad saw this, he started laughing and steered with his knee and waved back to us with both arms out the window.

We stopped for lunch and my mom reprimanded all of us, my dad included. "Timbo (by now they had dropped the Timmy crap for the more age appropriate *Timbo*) could have lost control of the car, careened off the road, landed in that swamp, probably upside down or worse, and all of you could have been eaten by the alligators here in Montana!" We could always count on our mom to come up with the most gruesome way for her kids, whom she loved, to die. Years later, after she died, Mike and Nan and I did wonder if she secretly yearned for our deaths just so she could get a little peace and quiet.

Along the way we learned that one of the partners in Dad's new business died in a plane crash. The remaining partner, who was the financial backer, told my dad to continue on and the two of them would start and run the company.

The business in Seattle was a success, so a few years later they decided to open a branch office in Portland. They decided my dad would get it up and running, and then manage it. That's when we moved to Lake Oswego.

CHAPTER 9

My allure vanishes

My drive to high school required a left turn to access the parking lot. At that intersection, looking directly ahead, past the crest of the road, if the weather was clear, a spectacular view of Mt. Hood presented itself.

MT. HOOD SUNRISE

When Mt. Hood appeared, I kept going straight up to the mountain to go skiing. My grades suffered.

Remember, we had a cabin on Mt. Hood and we kept all our ski gear there. It took just a few minutes in the cabin to change my clothes and grab my skis. Within thirty minutes I'd be skiing at The Ski Bowl. We had season passes so it just cost me the gas money to get to the mountain and back.

The Ski Bowl consisted of, creatively, the Lower Bowl and the Upper Bowl. The Lower Bowl was perfect for hackers and gapers: damn near flat. The Upper Bowl offered some of the steepest terrain and most challenging lines on Mt. Hood.

Mt. Hood is not powder country. The Bowl's base is only 3,500 feet above sea level so the snow is consistently rain soaked bat guano.

The storms would roll in from the west, dump a shitload of snow and then, it would warm up and rain on top of the new snow. If luck was on your side, the storm would pass in the afternoon, the clouds would part, and the cold night would produce a solid two-inch layer of frozen crust on top of the glop snow. Perfect conditions! First tracks? Few dared. Those of us who did make first tracks ended up with painful, black-and-blue bruised legs, just below our knees.

Learning to ski in that crap turned out to be a blessing. We in the Northwest never experience real powder snow.

It never gets cold enough or dry enough. We know what breakable and unbreakable crust is. We know what slop, frozen slop and bat guano are. We are masters at skiing crud.

Skiing is all about practice. Put more mileage on the skis and you can't help but get better. I got to be a very good skier. I was a ski instructor during my junior and senior years in high school. I first joined the ski race team but after standing at the top of the course, in the rain, for three hours I decided it was not for me and got the ski instructor gig that same day.

There were a few other kids who went to other high schools and also skied during the week, instead of going to school. I rarely dated girls from my school. When they discovered I was not around on the weekends to take them out, my allure, such that it was, vanished.

CHAPTER 10

Zeke nearly gets creamed

R arely did I drive the same way to high school and back. I made it a point to take the most indirect route so I discovered many obscure roads around Lake Oswego. Most of the roads in Oswego wind around and have few straightaways. On the way home from school in the late fall of 1964 I saw Zeke, in his wheelchair, in the oncoming shoulder waving his arms frantically.

I recognized him immediately. I'd given him a ride home a couple of times and he lived close by. I slowed down and pulled my car over onto the side of the road, got out and hurried over to see what the fuss was all about. He was very frightened, upset and having a tough time getting his words out. I tried to calm him down as he was sobbing and shaking uncontrollably.

"Jezus Zeke, slow down man, relax, take a couple of breaths and tell me what happened." His speech was difficult to understand on a good day. This was not a good day.

I began to get his drift and helped him, slowly, piece together what had happened. Apparently some jackass had attempted to run him down or at least scare the shit out of him by taking aim at him in a car and swerving in his direction. The car barely missed him then skidded back and forth across the road in an uncontrolled slide, missed the corner up ahead and flew off the edge of the road and wrapped itself around an old growth fir tree.

"Whoa," I said, "we better take a look. Maybe the people in the car are hurt."

I rolled Zeke towards the sharp left hand corner. We both took note of the long skid marks that originated just past where Zeke had been and continued wildly from one side of the road to the other. The skid marks ended where the car flew off the road to the right.

All the brush on the shoulder was completely torn out. The roadside alder saplings had been pushed over or were sheared off about five feet above ground level. I stopped to check it out. I looked down and saw a familiar bright red Mustang that had slid down off the embankment and rolled up on its top and lodged itself against a large Douglas fir tree. The wreck was about thirty yards down a steep embankment. I stumbled down the hill to see if the driver and any passengers were OK.

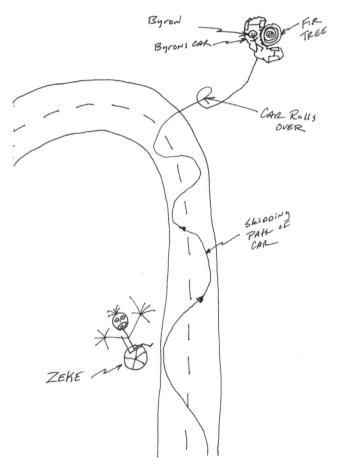

Byron
Byron's car
FIR TREE
CAR Rolls OVER
SKIDDING PATH oF CAR
ZEKE

BYRON'S CAR WRECK PATH

I was not expecting survivors as the car was a mess. It looked like it had rolled over at least once as every side was bashed in and all the glass was busted.

The driver was alone and badly hurt, covered in blood, his jaw lay at a grotesque angle.

"I'm trapped, please help get me the fuck out!" he begged.

Well, he's conscious. I guess that's good.

He was sprawled upside down and caught between the crumpled top and the seat. He was flattened. The steering wheel had collapsed around his legs and held him fast. Both of his legs were splayed at differing odd angles and each looked to be mangled and badly broken. He was unable to move them.

It took me a few moments to recognize him from high school. It was Byron Hydros, the mean bully and all around fucked up asshole. I had some history with him and his mean spirited personality which I'd learned about from Lucy. She also knew that his dad, Delbert, beat his wife and had sexually abused all his kids, including Byron, for years. Byron was an asshole, no getting around that, but I also felt sorry for the guy. He was fucked up inside through no fault of his own but like Lucy said he was turning into his dad, or worse.

CHAPTER 11

The title of this chapter is longer
than my high school football career

For some bizarre reason, I went out for football my freshman year. That turned out to be a really stupid idea. By then I was almost five feet five inches, and on a big day tipped the scales at nearly 139 pounds. My legs were strong from skiing but my upper body was mostly flab and underdeveloped. First day of practice, I suited up and ambled out to the field for our first meeting with the coach. I was stunned; standing there, all 350 pounds of him was the coach, Delbert Hydros, Byron's dad. After hearing about what a monster this guy was through Lucy, I doubted if I could put up with knowing about him and stay on the team.

He gave an annoyingly long speech about staying healthy for football. He told us, "Football is now the most important thing in your lives and you will give up any activity that poses any risk of injury that might deter your football career."

Rolling my eyes and thinking to myself, "Not only do I have zero respect for this genuine asshole; he's fucking nuts if he thinks I'm going to give up skiing." If anything, I would give up football in a heartbeat to keep from getting an injury that kept me from skiing.

During that afternoon's scrimmage I was on the defense when the QB lofted a beautiful long pass down the sideline and some talented kid caught it and streaked across the goal line. I was about thirty-five yards behind, running as fast as I could, a slow jog, along the sideline. I had no chance of catching the kid, besides he was already in the end zone, but thought I should, at the very least, show some effort. I remember seeing a flash out of my left eye the moment I got creamed.

I came to about ten yards off the field with Byron, who outweighed me by a solid eighty pounds, glaring down taunting and laughing at me. "You little puke, whenever you dare to go after my receiver I'm gonna split your fucking head wide open!"

Fuck me, this guy is crazier than I thought. I'd seen him as an ignorant bully but never this, the-wild-eyed-out of control lunatic that Lucy described. All I could think was, "Why? What the fuck is wrong with you?" Lucy said he had a sweet side but right then that seemed pretty far-fetched.

A couple of the other guys on the team ran over and pushed him away from me. Byron flipped out and went into one of his a blind rages cursing wildly and swinging at them with his fists. Coach Hydros waltzed over, hit Byron hard across the back of his helmet and told him to shut-the-fuck-up and settle down. "I'll deal with you later shit-for-brains." Then he turned to me and asked, "Are you OK?"

I regained my senses enough to ask him, "What the fuck just happened?"

He chuckled, "That boy of mine is just over enthusiastic sometimes."

"Over enthusiastic! Over enthusiastic! Your god-damned pervert kid damn near killed me and you're laughing? Go fuck yourself," I seethed.

A couple of the guys helped me to my feet and led me back to the dressing room. I ripped off the football costume and never thought of playing football again. To this day I'm not much of a football fan. I don't take pleasure in seeing people getting hurt.

Coach Hydros was also my history teacher so my grade at that moment may have slipped even lower, if possible, due to my direct, succinct language. Turns out the fuck-for-brains had been beating his wife and abusing his kids, including Byron, for years.

Football season started and Lucy wanted to go to a game and she wanted me to take her. "I'm going to the football game Friday night and you're taking me." She had a way with words. There was not enough snow in the mountains yet so I couldn't use the, "Sorry, I'm going skiing," excuse. Damn!

Reluctantly, I drove over to her house to pick her up. I knew Lake Oswego well, but it took me two tries to find her house. It was the only joint on a little, hard to discover, lane. I was greeted by an imposing ten foot tall solid brick wall. I couldn't see the top but I bet it was festooned with broken glass. Jezus! I was surprised there were no armed guards. I pulled up to a huge gate which slowly opened. I followed a long circular driveway which eventually led me to the front door. Actually, it was more like a grand entrance. This place was like no other in Oswego. This wasn't a house, not even a mansion, it was a fucking palace! I parked and walked to the door, which opened before I had a chance to knock. Her dad answered, saw me, looked over his shoulder and politely told Lucy, "Your date is here."

"Dad, he's not my date, he's just a friend."

He turned to me and shrugged as if to say, "Oh, just a friend? That's got to be tough to hear." He looked up and saw the shit beige plonker station wagon, looked back at me and sarcastically uttered, "Nice car."

Lucy came to the door, looked at the car then back to me, and in a mocking tone of voice grumbled "The El Crappo wagon?" Chuckling, "So Daddy wouldn't let you drive the yellow Impala?"

"Nope, my folks drove it to the country club for some golf awards dinner thing."

"Oh well, the wagon it is. Better than walking," as she whacked me on the side of the head with her cast.

Her dad called out to us, "You kids have fun at the game."

When some sympathetic fans saw Lucy's arm in a cast they scrunched together to make room for us in the first row of bleachers. Lucy and I took a seat which was right behind our team, the Lake Oswego Lakers. While we were waiting for the game to start, Byron, in his comical looking football regalia, saw us out the corner of his eye. He wheeled around unsteadily, and starts giving both of us shit.

Loudly slurring at Lucy, "What the fuck you doin' here with that little piss ant quitter?" The sympathetic fans moved further away from us.

"He's drunk," she whispered to me, "and that is definitely not good. He goes off the deep end when he's drunk."

Fuck, just what I need, showing up at a football game with Lucy and her drunk lunatic boyfriend eager to go psycho at any moment, on me.

First play after the kickoff Byron creamed some poor guy on the other team after the whistle. The ref threw a flag in Byron's general direction and Byron flipped out. The ref picked up his flag and calmly walked away when Byron charged after him screaming God-knows-what in the guy's ear. Apparently Byron, in his uncontrolled heightened state of rage, yelled the wrong thing at the ref who, without hesitation, turned and threw him out of the game. Delbert, our esteemed coach, waddled onto the field screaming and waving his arms just as Byron punched the ref in the nose. The teams converge, the refs converge, then Delbert punched one of the refs in the stomach and all hell broke loose. Total mayhem.

DELBERT HYDROS, A1 DICKHEAD

I turned to Lucy and said cheerily, "Now this is my kind of football!" By now the principal of the school had rushed onto the field and got right in the middle of this debacle. Finally Delbert realized that Byron was drunk and kicked Byron off the team. The principal fired Delbert on the spot when he discovered Delbert is also drunk. You just can't make this shit up!

With her eyes wide open Lucy turned to me, "Jezus!"

"Yeah, no shit! Kind of makes me proud to be a Laker, how about you?"

She cracked up. "One play into the game, what do you say, shall we get the fuck out of here?"

"Yep, I've had more than enough of this shit. What should we do?"

"I don't care; just get me out of here."

The next day somebody ratted out both Delbert and Byron to the cops.

Three days later, four squad cars showed up at the Hydros residence. They arrested Delbert, cuffed him and dragged him out to one of the cop cars while the whole neighborhood watched.

I wasn't there but Evelyn, Delbert's wife, told Lucy, "He was sobbing like a five year old and screaming."

"I'm coming back and, swear to God, I'm going to kill you and all your fucking kids!" Apparently Delbert said this, in a blind rage, a number of times, unaware there were eight policemen in attendance. That made his defense in court, "She made me do it," a tad thin. He got twenty-three years to life in the state penitentiary for a long list of counts including but not limited to spousal and child abuse. He had been a busy boy. Byron went to court a couple of months later. All he got, as a juvenile, was two years' probation. Fuck me.

CHAPTER 12

How I save Lucy and fuck myself

Back to Byron being stuck in his Mustang. I have to admit it was a cool car, bright red, a fastback with a 289 cubic inch V-8, four speed, nice tires and mag wheels. Blisteringly fast in a straight line but it defined what a truly shitty snow car could be. It was of absolutely no interest to me. Seeing it wrapped around that tree was still a sad sight.

Byron thought he was cool and tough, but most of the kids at school saw through his bullshit and hated him. Now he was in a situation he couldn't bully his way out of.

He must have been hurting, but still had the nerve to scream at me, "Get me out of this car you little piss ant whimp."

Kneeling down and getting right in his face I spoke quietly, sarcastically, "Byron, Byron, Byron, you don't remember me do you?"

His eyes grew wide as he began to recognize me, "I know you, you're the Tard tutor. Thank God you showed up, please help me get out of this car. I can't move my legs," he whimpered.

BYRON'S RED MUSTANG

"Hey, we have a grand prize winner!" I
knelt down and quietly whispered, "Yeah Byron
I'm the guy you unnecessarily creamed on the
sideline. I'm the guy who tutors the physically
and mentally disadvantaged kids. You know the
ones you take such delight in bullying because
they can't fight back. I'm also one of the many
people you bully and all of us could care less
if you live or die but until just now none of us
had the opportunity to make that dream come
true."

"I don't give a fuck who you are," he spewed,
"just get me out of this fucking car right now so I
can beat the shit out of you. I'm sorry I hassled
the kids at school. If you help me get out of this
car I promise I'll never bully them again."

"Fuck you Byron. Lucy told me everything about you. How you hit her, how you
pushed her down the stairs broke her arm. How
you raped her."

"That bitch had it coming! Now get me
out of this fucking car so I can beat the shit out
of you," he howled.

"Lucy told me all about how your dad messed with your little brother and sister. He beat your mom and wouldn't let her out of the house. He started fucking with you when you were just four years old. He's a monster and you're just like him, maybe worse."

"My mom hated him for no reason and made his life hell," he growled. "Please, for the love of god, help me get out of my car. I'm sorry I treated Lucy so bad. I love her, but sometimes she says shit that drives me crazy. I'll never hurt her again, I promise."

"You're right about that bucko. You're never going to change for the better. You're just like your sicko dad."

"Hey Byron, you smell that? Smells like gas to me! Man, that would be a shitty way to go, especially at such a young age. What are you, seventeen? Got held back a couple of grades eh? Getting burned to death in your own car, now that would be a shitty way to die especially at such a young age. Talk about karma."

He continued to howl and blubber at me to get him out of his car. He was getting pretty agitated by now. Animated. Desperate. I just calmly knelt there.

"Byron, I asked you over and over to quit hassling the kids, but did you? Fuck no, in fact you doubled down each time I asked and gave them an even harder time day after day. You really aren't that sharp are you?"

"I said I was sorry and I won't ever do it again!"

"Do you understand that most of the kids in school will be happy to hear of your demise? Wow Byron, that smell of gas is getting stronger. Did you happen to just fill up the tank? What's this thing hold, fifteen gallons?"

He kept screaming at me in a terrified voice to get him out of the car. I remained kneeling right in his face.

"I can't think of a single person, maybe even your own mother, who wouldn't like to hear of your grisly death. Being burned alive in your red fucking Mustang, how apropos. Hey did you know I smoked? Not very often but from time to time I like to burn one, like now."

His eyes grew wide as I pulled the pack of butts and a book of matches from my shirt pocket. He started crying and pleading some unintelligible bullshit while helplessly thrashing around in the car.

"When I get out of this car, I'm going to kill you!" he squeaked. "Oh dear God, don't do it. I'm so sorry, really I am. Please help me."

"Guess what fuckwad, that ain't gonna happen" I said savagely. "Your days of bulling me are over." In that moment he understood I was going to light the match and there was nothing he could do to stop me. He grew very quiet, his rage evaporated in front of my eyes.

"Go ahead then, do it, light the fucking match. I'm fucked up. I'll end up being a bigger monster than my dad. I hate myself. I don't want to live this way, but I can't help it." He looked me straight in the eye, "Do it, light the fucking match right now you little chicken shit. I dare you."

I looked him straight in the eye and, with a sick smile, I casually lit the cigarette and gently tossed it and the burning match into the back seat.

As I backed away, watching the flames lick at Byron who was screaming bloody murder, the car exploded. I was ten feet away when the force of the explosion hit me. I got blasted about fifteen yards further back where my head struck a tree and knocked me cold.

I awoke to a couple of firemen pulling me further away from the fireball. I was taken aback by the extreme heat coming from the Mustang. It was raging, fully engulfed in flames. I saw Byron in the car. He didn't look good. Toasted. He had that frozen in place look that reminded me of the corpses left in Pompeii. Ironically, the exact subject we had been studying in history class. Mt. Vesuvius, clouds of ash killing thousands, you know that history stuff. Fucker got what he deserved.

I glanced up and saw Zeke in his chair along with a small group of people who had stopped to see what was going on.

They were now standing on the side of the road transfixed by the nightmare scene taking place in front of their eyes.

I slowly opened my eyes and a firemen standing over me asked if I was OK. I didn't know it then but my eyelashes were gone. My eyebrows were gone. My hair was melted. My face and arms were badly burned and my head was badly cut where it had hit the tree. The firemen quickly wrapped my head (twenty two stitches at the hospital) and helped me clamber back up to the road while the rest of fire crew was putting out the flames.

A cop came over and asked if I had been a passenger in the car.

"No, but Zeke and I were the first on the scene and I was trying to get Byron out of the car when it blew up."

"Byron?" The cop asked somewhat surprised. "You knew the guy?"

"Yeah, his name was Byron Hydros and he went to my high school."

"Hydros? We all know about those dirt bags. In fact, I was the one who cuffed Delbert and put him in the squad car. Nobody's gonna have to put up with his bullshit for a long, long time. Looks like Byron got just what he deserved too, stupid motherfucker."

Sitting there on the side of the road it hit me. Jezus, I'd just killed a guy in cold blood, well cold blood may not be the accurate term, but I

POLICE ARTIST SKETCH OF CROWD

murdered him. No getting around that. I was in shock, dazed and felt nothing.

Zeke saw it in my eyes. He witnessed me light the match.

I didn't feel much for weeks. I wandered around in a dazed state. I saw Lucy in ceramics class and we hung out from time to time, but our conversations were muted. She looked good; I was just beginning to realize how good she did look. More importantly, she seemed happy, like I'd never seen before.

* * *

Twenty years later I was living in Sun Valley and skiing nearly every day during the winter. One morning I made five or six runs and headed to the Roundhouse for my mid-morning latte. I was sipping and gazing out the window, completely lost in the view of the Pioneer mountains to the east.

From two tables away I heard, "Tim? Tim Neun, is that you?"

The voice was familiar. Something from my past rang a bell. I looked up and could not believe my eyes, "Lucy, is that you?"

"Yes, it's me, Lucy, from ceramics class! What are you doing here?"

She picked up her coffee and sat down across from me.

I was stunned, "I live here, what are you doing here?"

"I just moved here and it's entirely your fault," Lucy said.

"My fault? Well, it is Sun Valley so you are welcome! You look great and it's wonderful to see you again. What made you move to Sun Valley? In high school you were a lacrosse player, not a skier."

"That's the part that's your fault. All you talked about in high school was skiing. You were the only guy in high school I trusted so I decided to try your sport. I started taking ski lessons at The Ski Bowl and fell in love with skiing."

I downed my latte and said, "Let's go make some turns so I can see how well the ski instructors at The Ski Bowl did."

"They were jerks, but in between hitting on me, I learned to turn and stop. Remember, my folks were wealthy, so I was able to ski all around the world and I got better. Like you said, 'It's all about mileage.' Sun Valley kept popping up in random conversations among strangers riding up chairlifts damn near everywhere I skied. I decided to see for myself what all the talk was about. So, five years ago I came here for a vacation. I became enamored with the Wood River Valley and knew I would move here. I bought a house last year and feel like I've finally found my home. My Idahome. It really is a magical place."

I suggested we take a run down Ridge while we were riding the lift to the summit. It's always groomed to perfection. Pretty easy, but I would get a chance to see her ski creds. She was good, really good. She liked to go fast and could really crank her turns. It was obvious she had put a lot of miles on skis.

We stopped at the top of Rock Garden and I told her, "You're a damn good skier. I'm proud of you!"

She smiled.

"Let's ski the Roundhouse south slopes down to the Cold Springs chair." I had skied it earlier when it was perfect corn snow. Now, two hours later, it would be six inches of sun baked bat guano. Another test. She cranked it with style, grace and power.

"You fucker, that was a test. How did I do? Remember, I learned to ski at The Ski Bowl so sloppy crud is my favorite."

"You're a great skier. More importantly you're a great crud skier!"

We made another four or five runs down the south slopes of the bowls. Our conversations on the chairlift rides were mostly about where to ski next, nothing serious.

We both had some work to do so agreed to meet later at the Pioneer for a drink and dinner.

That evening we sat at the bar in the Pioneer and, right off the bat, she asked, "So tell me your life story."

"I'm a loner. I tried marriage but we fell out of love at about the same time and I've been single since. There are big parts of my life I don't share which makes a meaningful relationship impossible. I work a little. In the winter I live here and ski. In the spring I work a little and ski mountaineer up in the White Cloud Mountains east of Stanley. I have a cabin up there I use as a home base. Summers I work and hike in the Swiss Alps. In the fall I go to my place in the Cook Islands and work and dive."

"Sounds like a lot of fun with a little work thrown in. What exactly do you work at?"

"Weird investments mostly. Stuff that is interesting but high risk. Most of the time they don't pay off, but when they do they pay off pretty well. Weeds out the cheapskate nosepickers. So, Lucy, what about you?"

"I handle my parents' investments. Sounds like we could be one of your clients soon."

"You know, I was asking about your real life. Married, kids?"

"Nope, no kids. I never got married. I've dated some, but I never let anybody get close. I've only had two second dates. I declined the third dates. My trust was destroyed after Byron. I'm incredibly careful around men; I will never let myself be used like that again. I'm single, and I'm OK with that. I don't mind being alone. I'm comfortable with myself. From time to time, I've tried to deal with my distrust of men. I worked with a couple of shrinks, both women, but it didn't help much. My time with Byron was traumatic and it left a scar that may not heal. I guess I'm not ready to forget about what can happen if I don't keep my guard up. My guard is always up. I can't tell who to trust, except myself. I haven't given up on the possibility of a relationship. The right guy might come along some time. Maybe I'll be able to drop my guard a bit. Maybe I'll be able to trust again. And, by the way Tim, I trust you. I always have."

"Lucy, I'm flattered you feel like you can trust me. I've always liked you, but there is a part of me I can never share, with anybody. You deserve more."

"O.K., I get it. Well, let's just try sharing the parts we can share. We can ski together. We like each other. Let's just leave it at that."

Tim Skiing

CHAPTER 13

300+ Empties in the back seat

Remember, I attended, at my leisure, Lake Oswego High School, home of the fighting Lakers; it was the swanky suburb of Portland, Oregon. I was not a stellar student. In fact, I was a lazy student. Studying? I had more important things to do. We lived on the lake and had a brown and white sixteen-foot Glastron fiberglass ski boat with a fifty horse power Johnson outboard. I spent the summers water skiing and goofing off on the lake with guys from school. Our friendship was based on the fact that I lived on the lake and had a boat. They always showed up with gas money, good guys.

I also spent quite a number of days during the summers ski mountaineering. There were only a few friends I trusted enough to go with. Mountaineering for us was to climb up steep parts of Mt. Hood and ski down. Don't fall.

The last six months of my freshman year I was not humming along at one hundred percent. I didn't understand that some long term, unease was to be expected after murdering someone.

My folks decided I needed something to snap me out of my malaise so they signed me up for Outward Bound. That's what they told me. My older brother and sister were out of the house living on their own so maybe Mom and Dad wanted me, the only kid left at home, to be out of the house for a few blessed weeks of peace and quiet.

The Outward Bound session I attended was a thirty-day program that took troubled city kids and me (privileged white kid, secret murderer) into the mountains and taught us how to become more responsible for ourselves and others. Perhaps it would give us the opportunity to look inward for strengths we had, but never been given the opportunity to discover.

Being in the mountains for thirty days would be hog heaven for me. I found myself really looking forward to participating. It was good to be thinking about something besides my recent past.

THREE SISTERS AND BROKEN TOP

This session was in the Three Sisters Wilderness Area in central Oregon, an area I loved and knew pretty well. It encompasses a number of massive glaciated volcanoes in the Oregon Cascade Range.

The first night out our guide/instructor, Rob, talked to us about how important trusting each other would become. Our very lives would depend on it. Our eyebrows raised in harmonious unison. Our very lives? Rob said a good way to start trusting each other would be for each of us to tell the others about our lives at home. We were sitting around the campfire. Rob told us that the rule was to not judge, or comment, just listen. The talking started slowly and those few with relatively normal upbringings were the most open and relaxed.

I didn't divulge I'd killed a guy six months earlier. Like me, most of the guys were guarded and only opened up a sentence at a time. We kept our vow to not judge each other. Hell, we were kids and the idea of judgment was beyond our comprehension. That sounded like the realm of adults.

I learned that a few of the guys had lives so foreign they sounded like they were making their shit up. It took me quite a while to realize they were telling the truth. It became apparent that it was really hard for them to open up about the crap they had been through. Abuse, yelling, weird sex stuff, being kicked out of their homes and forced to live on the streets. Never, not just occasionally or on a whim, but never, going to

Tim Neun

school. These guys were sharing tales of life with drug addicted parents and having to live with a brother, sister or their grandparents.

Hell, my biggest dilemma, besides killing Byron, was the angst of choosing the proper ski wax. The guys cracked up and shook their heads in disbelief. It was a light hearted bonding moment which quickly passed.

As I listened to their gruesome stories, I was shaken to the core. I knew this shit happened from what Lucy had told me, but to this extent? How do they put that horrendous shit aside and live life? Talk about being sheltered to the evils of the world. Fuck! I gained an appreciation for my mom and dad right there and then. Sadly, I never found the words or took the time to express my appreciation to them. I grunted out a "thanks" from time to time. They seemed to understand. Then they passed away.

The campfire conversations felt forced. More came out in random bursts at odd moments. We were on a fast march to the base of the South Sister and the two the guys behind me were talking about both their moms being prostitutes. I had a vague idea what a prostitute was; it had never crossed my mind that prostitutes had kids. They weren't allowed in the house after school. Dinner? Tough shit kid, you are on your own. Dads, if even around, were drug addicts. Needles, heroin, overdose deaths, guns. Jezus!

These were good guys who got dealt a shitty hand, just like the *Crips* in high school. This Outward Bound experience was far removed from their normal lives. This was a serious immersion into a world they had never imagined. They were learning to appreciate all that being in the mountains can offer. The silence. The absence of people. Becoming accustomed to feeling insignificant and appreciating being immersed in such a vast, new world.

At the beginning they were completely out of their element, but caught on surprisingly quickly. As the session continued, I learned they were for the most part tough, smart but troubled kids, who couldn't deal with their screwed up lives. It didn't look like they had any kind of normal future. I thought some of them might follow in the footsteps of their screwed up families. No wonder they were tormented. Among them there were a few who were already sideways with the law and were ordered by some judge or counselor to Outward Bound. This was sort of a last chance to turn their shit

SAME FUCKIN' LAKE WE PASSED TWO HOURS AGO!

Tim Neun

around before they were sent to *juvy*. Juvy was the junior joint.

First day we hiked fifteen miles. The next day, twenty. Little did we know Rob took us on the most indirect, circuitous route possible to the base of South Sister. Twice I pointed out, "Hey, we hiked past this same fuckin' lake two hours ago."

At first we struggled and complained but within a couple of days we got with the program and tolerated it. We were in some of my favorite places in the mountains. We started out by hiking up the South Sister, spent a few days rock climbing at Obsidian Cliffs, scrambled up the Middle Sister and had to actually climb the North Sister. We had to depend on each other for our lives when we were climbing. This was quite the learning experience for all of us and each stepped up to the challenge admirably. Nobody died and nobody got hurt.

SOUTH SISTER

We began our *climbing* adventures with the South Sister, the base of which we would reach the next day. It offered no actual climbing as there is a trail to the summit. A trail! No sweat! Actually, lots and lots of sweat. The South Sister is the third tallest peak in Oregon at 10,358'. Hiking to the top is a fucking grind. The trail gains 4,900 vertical feet in eleven miles up a steep, long, rugged trail.

This old volcano is a giant pile of loose cinder, dust and lava rock, just like all the other peaks in the Cascades. There are a few shear monoliths floating around. One area, Obsidian Cliffs, is an enormous region. We got to know a very small part of it intimately.

Eight guys pounding up a dusty trail means we were all moving along in a cloud of volcanic ash and dust. Under a microscope volcanic ash looks like ground up glass which, essentially, it is.

"OK," Rob said, "this dust is bullshit! Let's give each other twenty feet of space and see if that helps." It didn't. Rob said, "Let's head for Prouty Glacier about a mile ahead and hike on it to get out of this dust."

Little did we know that the, "Let's get out of this dust idea," was orchestrated ahead of time. Rob's plan was to get everybody comfortable with crampons, ice axes and ropes on the Prouty Glacier before we tackled the Middle and North Sister.

We spent a day and a half on Prouty Glacier. It's named after Joshua Prouty, a bone head pioneer MoMo who gallantly strode up about one hundred feet in cowboy boots, lost his footing, duh, took the slide of his life to his grisly death on the sharp rocks below.

Why do we white people name shit, like amazing, beautiful glaciers, after some religious idiot? We just change the whole fucking story to hold him up as some brave fuck-for-brains who helped conquer the west. I wonder what the indigenous folks called this glacier.

I also wonder how many other historical stories have been rewritten so many times that any shred of the truth has vanished. The Bible?—Nah!

I had limited experience climbing snow and ice on Mt. Hood, so I was familiar with the gear but, to be honest, I was a rank beginner. I had climbed Mt. Hood and done some ice climbing, so I knew how to belay someone on a climbing rope. The thing we all had to learn was to trust the guy on the other end of the rope. Did these city kids deserve my trust? They

12 POINT CRAMPONS

were on the other end of my rope belaying me. It took a while to feel assured they weren't fucking around when my life was in their hands and, I'm sure, vice versa.

Rob intentionally lead us to a very steep section where we practiced self-arrests while on belay. He wanted us to test ourselves and learn the skills quickly. The values of these skills became obvious. The base of this glacier, (where one would quickly end up, like Joshua Prouty, in an uncontrolled slide), culminated in large, sharp volcanic boulders. Another possibility was that we could fall into a crevasse. Certain Death. We quickly learned there was no screwing around without serious consequences. This was serious shit and every guy wised up right away.

Rob split us into teams, got us roped up and made us go through some basic belay techniques. Poor guy had nine kids on a serious glacier festooned with sharp pointy crampons, sharp pointy ice axes and tangled ropes tied in knots never seen by most of them. He was in the middle of everything yelling, "On belay, off belay." All the teams worked simultaneously. Again, amazingly, nobody died.

We camped for two nights next to the Prouty Glacier at around the 9500' elevation. It was just below the summit of South Sister at a bivy site Rob had scoped out while we were practicing on the glacier. We had a beautiful day for practice and the view was never ending. A cloudless, bluebird day in the cascades is highly unusual. Two in a row is miraculous.

Tim Neun

By the time we set up our tents that first night, made dinner, and had a short meeting about tomorrow's plan the sun set at our bivy site. It began to get chilly. The wind picked up and it went from slightly chilly to fucking cold. At least our site was flattish, though not smooth. We bedded down on a surface covered with sharp, fist sized lava rocks.

Our issued sleeping pads were not up to the task. They were crap. Thank God we were young and exhausted.

I tucked into my sleeping bag with every stitch of clothing I had, stuffed my boots in next to me and twisted my body around the rocks to find a comfortable position. I never did find one. It promised to be a long, chilly night. I pulled my arm out of the warmth of my sleeping bag and pulled the tent door to the

BIVOUAC

side and gazed out at a view that made it worth the misery.

The setting sun illuminated the west flanks of Broken Top, Mt. Bachelor, Mt. Thielsen and Mt. Shasta in the far distance. No throngs of people. No buildings, no cars and no sounds of humanity. The perfect opportunity for a life altering experience. Sure, it was cold, and I was lying on a bed of sharp rocks. O.K., forget the bullshit woo woo crap.

I awoke after what must have been nearly five hours of thrashing around non-sleep. Rob was banging pots and pans to announce breakfast. He was laughing and thoroughly enjoying waking us up at 4:30 am. Jerk. Later, I saw his sleeping pad. It must have been twice as thick as ours and the fucker slept like a baby every night.

I poked my head out of my tent, "Fuck me; it's still dark outside, and cold!" At that moment I looked up and saw stars, nothing but countless stars. As Carl Sagan said, "Billions and billions of stars." Nothing but a sky filled with zillions of stars. The starlight was amazing. I could see everything as clear as day. Our bivy was bathed in starlight. Then I looked up and saw the summit. I'd seen the stars like this before while in the mountains and each time it took my breath away. Wondrous. Beyond description. O.K. the bullshit woo woo shit is back.

The other guys were stirring in their tents and loudly cursing, "It's still fucking dark out and it's still fucking cold!" Rob told them to look up at the sky. There was dead silence followed by, "Fuck me, you guys, look at the sky; it's nothing but stars. Get up you guys; you've got to see this shit!"

We stood outside our tents looking up, not moving, and freezing our asses off. Being on the mountain and seeing the summit of the South Sister lit up with starlight along with the world below us aglow was mind-blowing. "Jezus, this is amazing," and, "No shit, and it's still really fucking cold out here."

I vaguely remember slogging to the summit of South Sister the afternoon of the second day on Prouty. When we reached the summit, we took a few minutes to take in the view before heading back down a different route that led us towards the Middle Sister. The guy next to me said, "This is nice. I've never seen anything so big." Another guy, slowly turned round and round taking in this magnificent view, "No matter what happens, I'll never forget this."

We hiked down from the summit and came across a beautiful flat, well-used bivy site with no rocks! Everybody was totally spent from the last couple of days and we all got a good night's rest.

"Rise and shine you dipshits, we've got a lot of ground to cover today to reach Obsidian Cliffs. Get up, let's go!" We ate another breakfast of what can best be described as cold gruel, with transparent powdered milk. The guys had learned to put their boots in their sleeping bags to keep them from freezing solid and so we put on our partially frozen boots. With stiff legs, we shouldered packs that felt like they had gained forty pounds overnight. We trudged onward and downward, off to our next goal, Obsidian Cliffs.

We scrambled down between two glaciers on the South Sister and picked up the Pacific Crest Trail (PCT). We would follow it north for about fifteen miles past the Middle and North Sisters then take a left and end up at Obsidian Cliffs.

This section of the PCT ran to the west and parallel to the Middle and North Sisters following the timber line. It was mid-June and the previous winter had been a big snow year. Much of the time we were hiking on top of firm, spring like, snow fields. Most of the trail markers were below the snow so we navigated with a compass and kept to the tree line for visibility.

It was a cool, cloudy day which worked out well as the snow stayed firm for easy hiking. We crossed a couple big lava flows which, without the deep snow pack, would have been like walking across a burning desert.

We came across a few climbers headed for the North and Middle Sister. They stopped and chatted with Rob for a minute or two about the conditions on the mountains then we went our separate ways. From the PCT trail, the Middle and North Sister were foreboding. We knew we would be climbing them both in a few days. They were fucking impressive. We could see the crevasses on the Renfrew and Collier glaciers which might be on our route.

We reached Obsidian Cliffs in the late afternoon. "Look you guys, dirt! We have smooth, soft, slightly damp dirt! We have actual logs to sit on as opposed to sharp automobile sized chunks of lava. It's not deep-freeze cold and there are no gale winds." A soft breeze drifted through the sparse trees bringing a wonderful woodsy smell. "For a bonus we have a creek! Fresh water that we didn't have to carry! We can just amble over and fill up our water bottles whenever we want. We can just pour it on the ground and waste it!"

The Obsidian Cliffs are only about three and a half miles from the old McKenzie pass road so the area sees a lot of day hikers in the summer. It was mid-June so the place, in our minds, was packed. We must have seen thirteen people in just two hours. The intruders were talking, laughing, you know, obnoxious, noisy humans. They were probably drinking our water! Fortunately, this was a big area and they gave us plenty of room. I heard a woman say, "What is that horrible smell?" One guy pointed, correctly, at us, and they moved about a half mile away. Maybe we should use some of that extra water on our pits. Nah! At last, peace and quiet.

Climbing at Obsidian Cliffs was not about rock climbing; it was another method Outward Bound used to instill trust in the group.

It was about trusting the guy who had you on belay. It was about tying a proper bowline knot. It was about communicating with the guy who held your life in his hands. Proper rock-climbing technique? Read a different book for that; there are number of great ones.

We climbed, we peeled off, and we belayed the shit out of each other. We slept on the soft, flat dirt like babies. We talked, not so much about the past anymore but what we could do in the future. Now we were more confident. We started to think we might be able to do damn near anything we wanted after we got back to real life. We talked about what we were going to change in our lives at home. Some guys talked about trying to make a home when they got back. Adult shit.

We talked about the immediate future while gazing up at the mountains we would be climbing. We worried about the crevasses; they were huge, gaping gashes in the glacier. They looked like they wanted to swallow us, which they would in a moment of inattention. After three days of climbing at the cliffs, we didn't worry about each other. We had each other's backs and trusted each other one hundred percent. We had accomplished the main goal of Outward Bound. Trust in ourselves and each other. A huge gaping crevasse? No sweat.

Rob eased into the role of advisor instead of leader. It was like it was all planned out. It was. As a tight group now, we discussed our options and made our own decisions.

We decided to break camp the next day after lunch and head for the base of the Middle Sister. Our plan was to hike/climb up until we found a good place to bivouac for the night then climb the mountain in the morning. Then we would descend, find another place to camp, closer to the North Sister, and climb the North Sister on the third day.

Rob chimed in and suggested we climb both peaks in the same day. He knew we could do it. He explained that it was a hell of a lot faster than summiting the Middle Sister, climbing all the way down, hiking to the base of the North Sister and climbing all the way back up again. We pulled out a topo map and checked it out. He pointed out a long ridge connecting the two summits. It was about 2,000 meters long. On the map it looked good. We trusted Rob for good reason; he had done that route countless times. Rob knew a good bivy site a couple thousand feet below the summit of the Middle Sister where we could sack out for the night. We could start for the summit early the next morning.

Before dawn (why does it always have to be before dawn?), we ate a quick breakfast, broke camp, and saddled up. Onward and fucking upward again. We made it to Rob's bivy site in the late afternoon and made ourselves at home. We settled in for another uncomfortable, cold night. We all missed the smooth, soft dirt and mild temps of the last few nights at Obsidian Cliffs.

We got up at (take a fucking guess) way before dawn and made it to the summit right at sunrise. There was a solid cloud layer that covered everything except the tallest mountains. They poked through the clouds and were bathed in bright sunlight. We were on top of the world. We followed Rob down the ridge he had pointed out on the map. It fell away on both sides for a long, long way. We weren't roped up so we made a point to not stumble or slip. We dropped into the clouds and visibility vanished. Rob said, "It's called being in the white room." We started to gain a bit of altitude and broke back into the sunlight. It was amazing what a sharp demarcation there was between zero visibility and the on hundred-mile vista in every direction.

When we reached the main route to the summit of the North Sister there was a very steep gully filled in with bulletproof hard snow and short pitches of vertical rock. This was climbing. We roped up and headed up the ice using our crampons. When we came up to the rock faces, we took them off.

Crampons on, crampons off, on, off, on, off, made the climb tedious. Despite the crampon situation, we made good progress. In four hours, we reached the summit. We spent about an hour up there congratulating ourselves. We felt like real mountaineers and we were all in great spirits. The view was indescribable, humbling. The sun was warm, and we had accomplished our biggest goal so far.

Tim Neun

"OK boys and girls," Rob laughed, "It's solo time! We need to get going. The descent is tricky down the north ridge. It's dangerous and may take us awhile. When we reach Collier Cone, we take a right and head east to the solo area. That's where the real fun begins."

The last event in Outward Bound is the solo. We each had to camp at least one half mile away from each other. We were supposed to build a shelter and collect and purify our own water for four days. We had a limited amount of food, near starvation rations for teenage boys. We were supposed to find supplemental food somewhere in the woods. Most of the guys were nervous. They thought they had never had to depend on themselves. That was wrong. They were experts at depending on themselves and probably had been from an early age. They just hadn't done it in the mountains and totally alone.

North Sister

I was at ease because I'd camped on my own a number of times. I had a pretty good idea of what to expect and how I could manage. Rest and boredom, that was it. I made my shelter of tree limbs stacked up against the base of a fir, checked out the available water and filled my bottle. Then I ate damn near my entire food supply. I crashed hard at four pm. It was dark when I woke up. I couldn't go back to sleep and started looking more closely at my map with my headlamp. I realized the little town of Sisters was only about twenty miles down the highway. HHMMMMM. Sisters had food and I had lots of time. After all, the challenge was to take care of yourself including food. I had a plan.

The hike to the highway was only about ten miles so I packed up my small rucksack with my last change of clean clothes. Before we headed out on our solos, Rob made a point of telling us he would be checking up on us. We would not know his whereabouts, but he would be close by. So, I left a note for Rob saying I was headed for a little lake about eight miles away for one night. There were about forty little lakes within that eight-mile radius, and I didn't give him a clue which lake was my destination.

We were given three matches for the solo which I thought was risky. Come on, this is the Northwest Cascades, a rain forest! I cut a couple of stitches in my shirt collar and stashed about twenty more matches in there. I had kept a $20 bill in my rucksack and strapped the giant Bowie knife my dad had slipped me onto my belt. I swept the ground around my camp before I headed off so I could see if Rob or some bear had visited while I was gone.

I took off at eight a.m. and made it to the highway by eleven a.m.

I stuck out my thumb and some trail weary climbers picked me up. We all smelled the same. I was in Sisters by noon. The little country grocery store was used by climber and camper types. I bought a package of hot dogs, a dozen eggs, butter, ketchup, a loaf of bread and some other non-nutritious but delicious food which I figured would make the rest of my *solo* pretty damn comfortable.

I stepped out of the store, walked over to the highway and stuck out my thumb. I expected to get a ride from some college girl or maybe a nice family on a camping trip. Then I realized that after twenty five days in the woods without a shower and draped in filthy clothes, I looked more like some juvenile delinquent as opposed to the clean-cut innocent kid I thought I was.

The Pacific Crest Trail ran along the west side of the North Sister and skirted about three miles from my camp. The trail-head was twenty miles up the road. I needed to get a quick hitch. After wandering down toward the edge of town with my thumb out and without an offer for two hours, I was getting desperate. I'd hitchhiked before and never had a problem. That was going to abruptly change, big time, very soon.

The first offer I had was remarkable. I noticed the car from a long way off because it was erratically weaving from one side of the road to the other. Not a good sign. I crossed the ditch on the side of the road to stay out of the way. The car slowed as it approached me and lurched to a stop about ten yards past me, damn near in the ditch. I approached slowly; this was the biggest piece-of-shit car imaginable. There did not appear to be an intact body panel; both the windshield and rear window were crazed with cracks. It sat on shitty bald tires and voluminous exhaust smoke completely encased the car. Fuck.

I had no intention of taking a ride from whoever was driving it. Then the driver's door flew open and the scrawniest, filthiest, seediest little puke I'd ever seen poked his head out. He yelled at me, "Get in." He repeated "GET IN NOW!" I wasn't sure what to do: run? Run where?

Step by step I walked up to the car apparently mesmerized. I saw the backseat first; it was overflowing with empty beer cans. There must have been three hundred empties back there. I was also overwhelmed with the knee buckling,

DOYLE'S BITCHIN' SHORT

unimaginable stink emanating from the car. It smelled like the scat from a thousand sea lions that had been left out in the sun for a couple of weeks. He was not a slave to cleanliness. Jezus fuck shit.

"Ah's Doyle," he said grinning through a mouth with only three teeth, none of which had ever seen a toothbrush. "Get in, if you want a ride."

Suddenly I came to. "Nope, I'll walk," I said firmly. I backed away and decided to hoof it up the road. I was ready to run to put some distance between us fast. He closed his door and leaned over to open the passenger door.

"Ah come on, I don't bite too hard," he coughed and laughed at me. That coughing and laughing seizure sounded like it might produce part of his lung. I saw red spray come out of his mouth and drip down the inside of the windshield.

I kept backing away and skirting around the car a little off the road. I kept walking. He drove up behind me and stayed on my heels as I speed walked up the road. I considered running away from the road, but as luck would have it, there wasn't any cover here. The pines were old growth and sparse for as far as I could see.

Pretty soon it was clear that he wasn't going to go away. Hell, I only needed a twenty-mile ride, thirty minutes max. I thought, "I'm smarter, younger, and stronger than he is. I have my knife for defense." It was on my belt, under my coat. I touched the handle to reassure myself. I had to get back to my camp before I was found out. "What could happen?"

I slowed down. He pulled even and opened the passenger door in front of me. I barely had one leg in when he lurched ahead into the road. I grabbed for anything to keep from falling out and ended up with a plastic Jesus bobble head doll in my hand. My heart was pumping hard.

"You fuckin' ripped my Jesus bobble head right off my fuckin' dashboard you little dickhead."

At that moment we damn near got creamed by a log truck. Its horn was blasting and it swerved wildly to avoid hitting us. Log trucks are not known for their quick maneuvering ability. It was miraculous we didn't get smeared all over the highway.

"Goddamn fuckwad," he yelled while flipping off the driver who stuck his arm out the window and with verve, flipped him right back.

"I know that truck. It's Karl's and that fucker's tried to run me down before! That fuckin' son of a bitch! I worked for those dickwad bastards as a choker setter building a pioneer road east of here. They fired my ass 'cause I was doin' a little meth. Fuck me! They were all a bunch of tweekers, but my ass gets fired! I was just trying to keep up, mother fuckers."

I'm sure Doyle and his car were well known locally. Both exceptionally one of a kind.

He started talking, yelling, mumbling, and squirming around in the driver's seat as the car wandered from one side of the highway to

Tim Neun

DOYLE

the other barely missing a couple of oncoming cars and another fully loaded log truck.

"Jezus fucking shit. Stop talking and look where the fuck you're driving," I screamed. Doyle never did stop talking.

Over the years I've come to understand that I am some sort of spiritual magnet who attracts *The Talkers*. You know, those folks who talk all-the-fucking-time! Is this some sort of cosmic torture I'm being subjected to? Maybe I'm the jerk because I can't just listen. Nah. I've asked around and many others are as annoyed with *The Talkers* as I am.

You have probably figured out by now that I'm pretty quiet, not much of a talker. I honestly do wonder how they keep it up. Being able to spew forth words in that unending flow, without a break, or any hint of a pause, is amazing. These are not talented orators. They just ramble on and on and somehow have the belief they know what the fuck they are talking about. They only need another person in the area to begin the talking spree. They don't want any feedback. There is a word for this malady: *logorrhea*. If you've read this far, then the term logorrhea, diarrhea of the mouth is a term you can use. Now you can up your language game right in the face of your illiterate, plonker friends by saying, "Fuck-me-runnin, that dip-shit has logorrhea."

For much of my life, I tried to listen. I tried to be polite. In the last few years have I been able to simply turn and walk away leaving them talking to air. It is quite freeing.

From time to time, I try to believe they have something interesting to say, but usually it is lost in the storm of words flowing from them and even they lose track of the point of the conversation (if there ever was one). I've realized, at last, that to them I am merely an animate object with ears. Ironically, I'm damn near deaf now. I tried hearing aids, but people's voices do not sound like people's voices. Everybody sounds like robots. Maybe it was just *The Talkers* I first heard with the hearing aids. Lord knows they sound like robots. Then it dawned on me that my world was getting to be wonderfully quiet. No ambient music, no Sonny and Cher, no logorrheans!

I've tried to break into their monologue, but *The Talkers* just talk louder and faster. They have absolutely no intention of having a conversation. It has taken me years to figure that out. Now when I'm hemmed in, sonically surrounded by one of these bozos, like I said, I just turn and walk away, guilt free. Try it! At first, I felt like a horrible person while walking away. "What an ass," I thought! But my rude behavior didn't seem to bother them in the least! When I happen to face that same person in the future, they look to be genuinely happy to see me. "Hey, there's Tim, I've talked incessantly at him before. I think I'll talk at him again."

It seems obvious they have zero self-awareness. They are boring the living shit out of everyone they encounter, unable to pick up on the subtle and not so subtle signs. I would like to challenge them with, "Hey, shut the fuck up, you are boring the fuck out of me!"

The logorrhean would probably hear that as an invitation and start again. "I'm glad you mentioned that as it reminds me of a never ending story that contains facts I just make up in the moment and plot lines that fade into oblivion and offer no deterrent to me to ever stop talking and I'm so glad you agree with me because I'm such a talented conversationalist and everybody loves me because I'm able to drone on forever." They just keep going. It is

KARL'S LOG TRUCK

astounding. How does one get this way? Is it a brain disease or just errant behavior they learned in their youth? In your snooty voice you point out (now that I've told you): it is called logorrhea, clinically known as I-have-to-keep-talking-or-I'll-die syndrome. Jezus, so die already or take some fucking pill.

Logorrheans lecture about everything they know, and they know everything, and they must let everybody know they know everything, always, forever. "I'm right and I'll keep telling you I'm right until you give up." They do have stamina. Logorrheans can string together unrelated drivel for hours, for days, for a lifetime. That's it. That is their life. They don't hear others. It must be a lonely life. Perhaps they look at me and think poor guy, he has so little to say, that has got to be a lonely life!

Are you tired of *The Talker's* rant yet? Lord knows, I am. It was my best attempt to sound like I had logorrhea. I'm bored to death thinking about them. That's it for the non-fiction portion of this book.

Let's move on. Back to my current predicament with a consumptive, drunk, logorrhean driver. Those aren't all of his contemptible qualities.

Doyle started laughing/coughing again and generated a giant, bloody lugie. He tried to launch it out the window, but it fell short and ended up on his already filthy shirt. He kept talking between coughing and hacking gobs of phlegm all over the inside of the car.

"I had three kids, a bunch of little fucking ingrates. My former psycho-bitch-from-hell wife caught me in bed with the oldest one so she took 'em all back to Kentucky. I've got a mind to go back there and kill that goddamn bitch. Fuck 'em, they ain't worth my time. Anyways I gots a new cunt wife, Darleen. She kicked my ass out today 'cause she thought I was getting a little too friendly with her twelve year old daughter, Fawn. Geez, she has no clue Fawn and me been fuckin' for a couple years already. I been showing the ropes to the other kid, Eileen. She's only nine, but looks fourteen and I can't stay away from them perky tits and little stiffy nipples and, hell, they love playin' with my pecker. Darlene can't stay away from it either. She'll take me back. You know, I've been known to let young boys, just like yourself play with my pecker," he said, "I could show you some shit that would blow your mind. Ever suck one of your buddy's cocks? Ever been fucked up the ass?"

Jezus fucking Christ, stop the fucking car and let me out! You're a fucking sicko pervert child molester and I want to get as far away from you as possible! I thought. I shouted, "STOP THE CAR AND LET ME OUT. NOW!"

He just laughed and coughed up more bloody phlegm and said, "I knows a good place to ditch you. It's just about five miles up this fuckin' road." He was only going about twenty mph which, per the tortured sound of the car, was about as fast as this piece of shit could go. At this speed I figured I could jump out and not be injured so badly that I couldn't get away from him. I kept watching for my chance, but wanted to get as far up the road as I could. My heart was trying to pound out of my chest.

He kept talking about fucking his wives and their kids. He bragged about killing one of the kids because he thought the kid was getting ready to snitch him off. He was either bullshitting me or was batshit crazy or both. I was scared like I'd never been scared before. I had to figure out what the hell I was going to do…and fast. Every minute in this car with this madman seemed like an hour. I should have run. At that moment I could probably have run the entire twenty miles.

We made it about fifteen miles further when he hit the brakes way late and careened off the highway onto a well-traveled logging road. He followed it for a couple of miles then turned onto an old spur road that was pretty rough. His piece-of-shit car bottomed out every time he lurched into the deep grooves in the dirt road. I knew exactly where we were. The Pacific Crest Trail was on the west side of this canyon. He careened onto an old landing and hit the gas instead of the brakes and crashed into the embankment. We hit so hard I bashed my head into the passenger window as my side of the car hit the embankment.

Doyle slid over the bench seat and slammed into me and the beer in his hand smashed into the other side of my head. He seemed unfazed. I was dazed. He was so close I could smell his breath. I tried the door. It was jammed.

"You little fucker, this is all your fault. God damn it anyway!" He drained the drops from the beer that was still tightly clinched in his left hand and grabbed my thigh in his claw-like right hand. We were eye-to-eye and I was trapped. "You gonna squeal like a little piggy?" he taunted. "You city-fuckers all the same, whining about some fucking owl and kicking us out of the woods. Now the woods are damn near shut down 'cause of you and your fucking striped or spotted or whatever the fuck your bird is." He was spewing spittle and sea lion breath on me with every logorrhean word. I was beginning to come around. I was shaking uncontrollably.

THE INFAMOUS SPOTTED OWL

He was getting more and more pissed off, muttering about the damn bird, the damn this, the damn that. All the while his grimy little hand was on my thigh.

He started to mutter again, "Gonna make you squeal like a little pig." All of a sudden I noticed he was rubbing his dick with his left hand. When the hell had he pull his cock out? pulled *

I was stunned. For a moment, I could not move. Without thinking, I reached around with my left hand and grabbed the Bowie knife. With all my strength. I whipped my arm around and thrust the knife into his chest. I held on to

Tim Neun

111

the knife; he let go of his dick. He looked at the knife, then at me, then back to the knife sticking out of his chest. He was speechless for the first time. He was dumbfounded. He realized this had not gone the way he had hoped.

Just to be sure he was disabled, I viciously ground the knife up and down then back and forth. I pulled it out with a surprisingly loud sucking sound and threw myself against the door and fell out of the car.

I heard him whine in a tiny voice, "Why did you do that? I was just foolin' round."

He puked blood all over the inside of the car and all hell broke loose for a moment or two then he made some gurgling sounds and everything grew quiet. I'd been listening to this shit-for-brains for over two hours and, I've got to say, not hearing his voice was wonderful. Sure, he was dead but at last it was quiet, deathly quiet.

The car was still running. I didn't want to touch it. I didn't want to have anything more to do with any of this shit. I started for the trail. Fuck, I just killed another guy. I'm only fifteen and I've already killed two people. Sure they were a couple of monster losers the world will be better off without but even to me that reasoning sounded shallow.

I stopped thinking about that philosophical bullshit after about three seconds. I was still shaking violently, and my heart was pounding. I shifted into high gear. I've got to get the fuck out of here and pronto. I ran as the crow flies up the canyon and came to the creek. I stopped and washed the blood off my face, hands and arms. My shirt and pants were covered in blood so I took them off, washed myself in the creek and changed into the spares I'd brought. I stuffed my bloody clothes into the plastic grocery bag and jammed it into my rucksack. I could still feel my heart racing, but I had stopped shaking. The familiar numbness returned and I knew I had to keep moving.

I kept running up the side of canyon towards the Pacific Crest Trail. I crossed the trail and turned to run parallel to it. I hiked with the trail off to my left and just in sight. I didn't want to run across anybody on that heavily used section of the trail. Off the trail about twenty yards away, I spotted a little patch of dirt hidden in the lava flow. I started a small fire and tore my bloodied clothes into little strips and burned everything I could. The rest I buried with the ashes under lava rocks.

The sun was going down and the evening light was fading as I came close to my camp. There was a half-moon so I could see well enough to continue to see where I was going. I only spotted two lights, either campfires or headlamps, and I gave them a wide berth and kept moving quietly towards my camp.

As I approached my camp, I stopped on a hill so I could observe the scene. I waited there for about an hour to see if Rob was near or might show up. When I was about to fall asleep on the hill, I silently slunk down to my shelter. I saw my note crumpled up on the ground. There was only one set of human footprints leading to, then away from my shelter. Hey, no bears!

I spent the rest of the solo wandering from lake to lake camping in obscure places trying not to think about what had happened. Rob never saw me as far as I knew.

When I showed up at the pre-arranged meeting place on the last day, Rob was relieved. He was also royally pissed. "I told you to stay close to your designated camp area. Where the fuck were you?" I mumbled some answer I cannot remember. I might have told the truth about exploring the lakes that were close by. Rob was more relieved than mad, I guess.

We hiked for two days back to the main Outward Bound camp. I remember almost nothing about the end of my experience.

My folks picked me up. They were glad to see me and were stunned at how different I looked. "You've grown up over the last thirty days, but you also look like you've been through hell." Little did they know! I never told them or anyone else.

I went back to Lake Oswego High School. Three years to go.

CHAPTER 14

1st Hangover,
Sony & Cher Squawking
I Got You Babe, @5:30 A.M.

Three years later, without anymore
drama except the normal already
described skipping, skiing, ceramics,
and not much dating, high school finally ended.
I did not graduate with honors. I squeaked out
with 1.87 GPA which was just barely good enough
to escape. My classmates were very excited for the
graduation ceremony. The caps, gowns, proud
parents. I could give a flying fuck. *Get me the
fuck out of here.*

On the next to last day of school, I said
my farewells to the kids I felt a strong bond to,
the crips, Lucy, a few guys, and Mr. Thornton.

I skipped the last day of school. I had
next to zero connection with most of my fellow
classmates. I could care less if I never saw any
of them again. I'd become a loner, a personality
trait I would carry throughout my life.

I headed up to our cabin on Mt. Hood
that day. I knew there was a big new ski area
being built over the summer and figured I
could get a job.

I showed up at six a.m. Monday
morning, found the office and told them I was

there to work. They asked about experience. High school, climbing, skiing, Outward Bound. "Hey," they said, "you are here, you are young, you look healthy, you are hired." Things were simpler back then.

I got a job as a grunt. I was a laborer. I joined other men digging the ski lift foundation holes. I was part of one of the lift building crews. We dug them by hand on the steep sections where equipment could not be used. Eight rocks, one shovel full of dirt. Ten rocks, one half shovel full of dirt. Mt. Hood is a volcano. Volcanoes are made from loose lava. I loved being on the mountain day and night. The physical labor was great. I did not have to think about anything too seriously. Just work.

At the end of my first day, after the last rock and teaspoon of dirt was taken from the current hole, we hiked down the mountain. We rode in a truck up the mountain in the morning. It was a bone shaking ride so hiking down looked faster and far more comfortable.

I strolled to my car and sat down to take my boots off. The guy parked next to me was doing the same. We struck up a casual conversation and learned we were both grunts, digging lift tower holes, but on different lifts.

I introduced myself, "Hi, I'm Tim, Tim Neun."

"Hi, I'm Dave, Dave Gast."

I looked into his truck, an old faded blue and gray International Scout that had seen better days. Inside were his sleeping bag, camp stove and all his shit.

DAVE'S SCOUT

"Are you staying in that?" I was six feet tall by then and he was taller than me and the back of the Scout looked to be four feet deep. "Doesn't look too comfy."

"Yeah, until I find a place to rent. It is a bit snug but when I put the tailgate down I can stretch out pretty well. It does get pretty cold at night."

"I'm staying at my parent's cabin in Government Camp. You could stay there. There's lots of room. Hell, we even have beds and heat!"

"Really?"

"Sure."

That's how I met Dave who has remained a lifelong friend. He followed me back to our cabin in Government Camp. We unloaded his truck and got him settled into the upstairs bedroom.

The cabin was always well stocked with tons of food thanks to my mom.

The cabin overlooked Govy (the affectionate nickname for the little town of Government Camp). I told Dave I was going to wander down to town to the phone booth and call my folks. I thought I should let them know where I was and that I had a job, and a roommate staying in the cabin.

I told them I'd met another grunt, Dave, who was planning to live in his truck so I invited him to stay at the cabin with me.

My folks worried about me for good reason. They were glad to hear I was staying in the cabin and working at Mt. Hood Meadows. My mom said she would buy more food. Moms, bless 'em. They would bring the food up over the weekend and come to see me.

My mom was thrilled. "I'll have to bring a LOT more food!"

My dad asked how the weather was. Winter in the Cascades continues through June and summer starts on July 4th. There is no spring. We do get a few beautiful teaser days, but usually the weather is cloudy, rainy and windy. It happened to be one of those rare, beautiful, spring days.

I told him, "It's another bluebird spring day, just like always."

He chuckled, "On those nice rare spring days I like to sit on the deck, sip some good Scotch and watch what's going on in Govy." I remained silent. Something was up.

"Tim, I know you water down the whiskey in the liquor cabinet. I notice it slowly turns to a light brown flavorless tea over time."

I gulped, "No, I didn't know that. I was hoping you wouldn't notice."

He let it go. "What you may not know is that I intentionally keep the shitty whiskey there just for you. How can you drink that crap?" he asked.

"Uh....I don't know."

He laughed and I heard him turn to my mom and say, "He keeps watering down the crappy stuff and continues to drink it. I overheard my mom laughing in the background "Oh, I know, poor, poor Tim."

"You can't serve that watered down swill to Dave. Go down into the basement and look behind the water heater. I keep A bottle of Glenmorangie Scotch there as an emergency backup. Try it! Hopefully, you will notice a difference. I've also got a humidor full of Cuban cigars hidden behind all the canned food in the cabinet above the refrigerator. You'll need a stepstool to reach them."

I knew about the bottle of whiskey behind the water heater, but it was sealed and looked expensive, so I let it be.

I did not know about the cigars and I thought I knew every square inch of that cabin. I did not know my dad smoked cigars and the Cuban part was especially surprising. They were conservative Republicans and Castro was a Ruskie, commie, pinko rat, rebel dictator with nukes pointed at the U.S. Cuban cigars seemed unpatriotic. At the end of the day they were capitalists which apparently made the expensive Cuban cigars okay.

Dad said, "Go get the good scotch and pour Dave and yourself a man-sized glass, relax on the deck, crank up the cigars and get to know each other."

Dad had made a point to talk seriously with me from time-to-time, but it had always been father-son stuff. This was the first man-to-man thing he had ever said to me. He was telling me to make ourselves at home, in his cabin, drink his good scotch, and smoke his Cuban cigars on his deck. I couldn't believe it. I was speechless.

"Tim, Tim are you still there?" Dad said.

"Yeah, I'm still here," I murmured.

"Good, you guys enjoy yourselves and leave me a sip or twelve of my good scotch. You know your mom and I love you and always will, right?"

"Yeah, like never before."

I hung up. Dave was standing there listening to my subdued conversation. He figured my folks were pissed and he would have to spend a few more nights in his truck. He was bummed but not surprised.

"No, just the opposite!" I told him what my dad had said.

He was as pleasantly surprised as I was.

"Jezus, that's amazing. What do you say we head back to the cabin and bust out that good scotch and light up those Cuban cigars?"

We sat on the deck, in the sun, looking down at the few people wandering around Govy, drinking my dad's special scotch and smoking his cigars. Neither of us had ever smoked a cigar.

We learned we both had just turned eighteen. He was from Belvedere, California, a small island in some bay in Marin County which meant nothing to me. He learned I grew up in Lake Oswego and we lived on the lake and it meant nothing to him.

Sipping and puffing away on those giant stogies was an amazing first. We felt like we were the most privileged grunts on the mountain.

"This is nice, eh?"

"I'll say!"

At that very moment in our shared superiority, we simultaneously lurched to the railing and puked our guts.

I could sense my dad, sixty miles away, laughing his ass off. "Oh Jack," my mom chimed in, "Silly boys," gasping for breath between bouts of laughter.

We crawled into the cabin and crashed. It was all of seven p.m. My radio alarm clock went off at 5:30 am. Squawking "I Got You Babe" by Sonny & Cher. It was a horrible shock. Sonny and Cher were always a horrible shock and the radio stations played their shit endlessly! I had never experienced a hangover before. It wasn't that bad, but coupled with the Sonny & Cher bullshit, I nearly puked. I turned the volume down, switched to the news and just lay there, moaning. The news was not good.

Every day more conflicting stories about the Vietnam War were in the news. Huge anti-war demonstrations were happening out there somewhere. Politicians' words divided the nation into believers and non-believers. I had my first hangover and I had to go to work and there was a war in Vietnam. Aggh.

That morning, our second day on the job, Dave and I looked like shit and felt worse. We drove up to the Meadows and crawled into the truck groaning loudly through the long bumpy drive up to the holes we were digging. The other guys quickly sussed our condition. They took advantage of us, teasing and yelling and screeching loudly "I got you babe" way out of tune. The driver hit the biggest rocks and potholes so that we were lurching more than normal. Finally, I had to roll down the window and dry heave which triggered Dave to do the same. The second day was starting off in a grand way.

I recognized Marv, the crew boss, as a lift operator I had seen during the winter at The Ski Bowl. Now he was the boss and it seemed like the *boss* thing had gone to his head. There were three ski lifts being built that summer so there were twenty or thirty lift construction grunts spread across the mountain. Sometimes Marv would spend an entire day with one crew, but usually he just drove a truck around and checked on the progress each crew was making. Marv's mode of leadership was limited to yelling, intimidation, and debasement: old school. By the end of the second day every member of every crew hated to see him coming. He had a reputation. He offered no leadership. He only made everyone's job harder. He yelled insults at every member of every crew. And yet he didn't know anyone's name. He called everybody either *Dipshit, Dumb-Ass* or *Girlie Hair*. Therefore, every member of every grunt crew quickly grew to hate him. He was the worst part of a good summer job.

Dave brought his ski equipment to the mountain even though it was summer. He knew Timberline stayed open for as long as the snow held out which might be mid August. He thought summer skiing sounded like fun. I did not tell him the summer lift, The Magic Mile, was as flat as a pancake. In fact, so flat it didn't matter which way you rode it.

He was scoping out my skis and pointing at one pair, asked, "What are these?"

"Those are my climbing/mountaineering skis," I answered.

"How do they work?"

So I explained them to Dave. "These bindings, an old pair of Silverettas, pivot at the toe so I can climb with the skins on the skis. The heel is free, that makes slogging up more like walking." I dug around in my rucksack and pulled out my skins to show him. "To ski down, you just pop off the skins and lock down the heels on the bindings and off you go."

Dave's eyes lit up, he understood the whole set up right off the bat. "Fuck, you can go anywhere, any time!"

He told me about his dad, Gary, who had been in the Army's 10th mountain division, the ski troops. "I've heard my dad talk about hiking and climbing with skins, but I didn't understand the lingo and the gear. That was twenty seven years ago and hard for me to imagine. I'm going to Portland next Saturday and buy a set of this equipment. Who sells it?"

"The Mountain Shop," I told him, "I'll go with you. I need to get some wax and a new raincoat. My folks are coming up Friday night after work to deliver groceries, meet you and go skiing on Sunday. We can blast down to Portland on Saturday to get all the stuff and we can mount the bindings when we get back. My dad has a shop in the basement, right next to the water heater. We can go skiing with my folks on Sunday and you can try out your new gear."

Mom and Dad arrived Friday late afternoon with the giant Biscayne wagon. It was packed to the gills with enough food to feed Dave, myself and most of Govy for a year. We carried grocery bag after grocery bag of steaks, pork chops, hamburger, chicken and one measly bag of carrots and put it all into the already fully stuffed freezer in the basement, right next to the water heater.

What the hell! The last thing in the car was a TV. Mom and Dad bought a new one, so

GIAGANTIC TV

they brought the old one up to the cabin. Keep in mind a TV, an old TV in 1967 weighed about 600 pounds. Having a TV at the cabin seemed sacrilegious. The cabin was a place to escape the bigger world. Mt. Hood, skiing, hiking, and the village of Govy was a world I knew, and it was comfortable. I was not sure I wanted the TV there, but I appreciated the gesture.

Dave and I ended up watching the TV in the evenings. The news was always about the war in Vietnam. The incessant noise was eroding the serenity of my sheltered mountain life. Fuck!

Two of the guys on the crew said they were going to join the army at the end of summer. "We gonna protect our country and

Tim Neun

kill some gooks while we're at it. Should be exciting!" That was the first time I'd heard that. They were guys I thought I knew because I worked with them every day. I thought they were joking. "We're not fucking joking. After the Commies take over Vietnam, they're going to attack America. Everybody knows that." I couldn't fathom it. They believed everything the lying politicians were saying. I did not realize people believed that crap and here were two of them right in front of me telling me like it was gospel. Seems like I am an atheist on a couple of levels.

My plan was to go to college in the fall so I would have a student deferment. I was not seriously thinking that the draft, the Army, or Vietnam would affect my life. The summer of 1967, I disbelieved what the politicians, the chicken hawks, Johnson, and the generals were telling us. Their lies seemed so obvious to me. They spewed all this bullshit all the time and so I truly did not understand people who took them seriously. It was quite a shock. Even fifty years later, it baffles me. The newspapers, radio, and TV were seriously questioning America's role in Vietnam with verifiable facts, not pandering bullshit like the politicians.

The U.S. just kept shipping more and more soldiers into the war over in Vietnam and throwing more and more lives away. They were using soldiers as war fodder. The soldiers, young men and women my age, were put in harm's way for reasons that appeared to be more infuckingsane every day. The soldiers put themselves in harm's way to be patriotic. They believed a bunch of fucking lying politicians who didn't give a flying fuck about them. Many came home badly injured. Many came home mentally wasted. Many never came home. The numbers kept climbing every day. Why? What for? For me, by then, summer of 1967, the War in Vietnam had no credibility.

After what seemed like years (thirty days), we were finally using explosives to blast the last holes for the group of towers at the top terminal. They were grouped closely together and only about thirty yards from the top.

Whenever we took our lunch break, we stopped working and found a spot to sit on a rock or the ground. Relaxing with lunch was a welcome break. Dave and I, per my mom's shopping, often feasted on ham and cheese sandwiches. We cut the ham extra thick, laid on good cheese, put on a slice of onion, and had mustard and mayonnaise dripping off the sourdough bread. We added a crunchy apple, a juicy orange, a banana. Lunch wise, we were the envy of the crew. Groaning loudly enough to ensure the rest of the crew could hear, "Man that was a great sandwich, probably the best I've ever eaten, even better than yesterday's! I'm fucking stuffed; I'll just leave the last of it for the chipmunks and squirrels."

Day after day the entire crew tossed their leftovers right where we sat. Everybody tossed their food scraps onto the ground for the chipmunks and the trash was thrown into whatever hole we were working on. We were a tidy bunch. Now you know when riding up some chairlift with your life depending on the integrity of the concrete foundations, that they are chock full of paper bags, sandwich wrappers, coffee cups, old lunch pails and busted thermoses.

TOP OF BLUE CHAIR

CHAPTER 15

I miss my opportunity to kill Marv. Dang.

It took us nearly a month to dig all the holes. Then the concrete guys came up and placed the rebar and tower bolts and tied them up with wire. The cement trucks were unable to reach most of the lift tower holes high on the mountain, so we poured the concrete using a helicopter. A large bucket was attached to the chopper by a one hundred foot long cable. The bucket contained about a yard of concrete. When the pilot positioned the bucket right above the tower hole, one of the crew would pull down on the release mechanism, a thing we called the *bail*, allowing the concrete to pour into the hole. The bail was a stout one inch diameter pipe that curved around the bucket.

While the helicopter hovered, nobody could hear anything, so we used hand signals between ourselves and the helicopter pilot. This let the pilot know when the bucket was in the right place, or if he needed to change position. The pilot could sense when the concrete was dumped per the lightened load but he waited for us to signal the all clear before he lifted and headed back down the mountain for another load.

HELICOPTER WITH CONCRETE BUCKET

Marv refused to learn the hand signals. He just shrieked loudly. No one could hear him. He waved his arms around frantically and everyone ignored him. We had to. Getting that bucket into the right place and signaling correctly to the pilot was hard work. We had to concentrate on the job at hand and we knew what we were doing. He did not. He was in the way and making our job more difficult. Our disrespect for him grew every day. The other crews were having the same problems with him: Dipshit Supreme. We knew his name.

To add difficulty, the bail started sticking. We told Marv about it and told him it had to be fixed. The next day it would not open without two guys reefing on it. We told him again, but he brushed us off. All the crews reported the problem. Maybe he wanted to look good by keeping on schedule or maybe did not believe it was any big deal because he did not trust any of us.

Another load of concrete arrived on the third day of the sticking bail and it hung up again. This time we could not activate it, no matter how hard we reefed, it would not budge. Marv had his head under the damn bucket looking to see why it was stuck. He motioned to us, "Pull it down," but it was still stuck. He kept waving his arms and howling to, "Open the bucket."

"It's fucking stuck again you dumbshit," I yelled back at him, sure that he couldn't hear me, but would get the intent. I felt the bail move just a little, but Marv's head was still under the bucket. He screeched at me again, from under the bucket, but I couldn't understand or see his head. Suddenly the bail snapped down, and unfortunately, it did not bash his fucking skull into about forty pieces because, simultaneously, he pulled his head out from under the bucket. It was a close one. The concrete dropped into the hole and we signaled to the chopper pilot. The chopper and bucket rose into the sky and headed back down for another load. Marv continued to scream at me.

Marv had lost his mind, "When I tell you to drop the fucking bail, you drop the fucking bail. Got it, Shit-For Brains?"

The other three guys had seen what nearly happened.

I looked Marv dead in the eye, and firmly growled back at him, "Trust me Marv, next time, I promise to drop the bail with everything I've got." And added under my breath, "No matter where you're stupid fucking head is."

CHAPTER 16

Sliced and Diced

As we reached the top terminal one morning, we leaped spritely from the truck. Today, while other crews worked farther down the mountain with Marv, the helicopter, and the sticky bail, we would be completing some holes. We looked forward to finishing up our blasting duties, maybe that very day. The hole only accommodated one lucky guy (we traded off) at the bottom. That lucky guy filled the bucket with rocks while another one of us hauled the bucket out with a rope.

As soon as we jumped out of the truck, we heard whining then some serious growling and hissing coming from our last hole. What the fuck? We looked down the hill and standing next to one of the holes was a cougar and two cubs. She was looking dead at us and she was pissed. What the fuck was a cougar doing this high up the mountain? Oh yeah, eating all the lunch scraps left by every guy on every crew member on the mountain. Once, while rafting the John Day River, I saw a cougar explode up a very steep five-hundred foot hill in five or six bounds. You don't want to fuck with a cougar. We froze. She was only about fifty yards away and the truck was further. Can I outrun the other guys?

As male human morons, we picked up rocks for protection and began yelling and throwing rocks at her. None of them came close, but at last she got the idea. She and her cub ambled over to a group of trees about fifty yards away. Before she disappeared, she turned and growled at us. She was not pleased.

We gathered up more rocks, and cautiously walked down to the hole she had been guarding. She continued to voice her displeasure. We looked and saw that one of her cubs had fallen into the hole. Perhaps he had gone a bit too far for a tasty morsel of ham. The cub was pissed and scared and wanted its mom. "Now what the fuck are we going to do?" we all thought.

COUGAR WITH CUB

EAR TO EAR

Marv showed up on the scene. Just what we needed. Our beloved boss said, "Let's just throw big rocks at it until we kill it then we can get back to work." What he meant was that we, the grunts, could toss big rocks into the hole and kill the baby cougar. That way he could sit in his truck, picking his nose, while the rest of us killed a baby cougar. Nothing should slow us down.

After putting up with Marv giving us a month of terrible advice and no real help while we were working our butts off, well, let's just say, by now, we all sincerely hated Marv. Like a dumb shit, I said, "Well Marv, if it were you stuck down in the hole, crying, I would be the first to pick up the biggest rock I could find and drop it right on your fucking head, crack it wide open, and then we wouldn't have to put up with your constant nose picking bullshit." That made me feel better! I just gave him a blank stare but, that is what I was thinking. Dave and several others gathered around giving him the evil eye. We weren't going to kill the baby cougar, so we ignored Marv and set to solving the problem in a non-Marv way.

Our first plan was to put the ladder in the hole. We figured a smart cougar would climb out and run to its mother. That didn't work. The baby cougar did not recognize the ladder as an escape.

"Fuck it, it's just a baby. It is only about the size of a healthy house cat. How dangerous can it be?" I said. I'd never spent much time around angry cats. "Well then, Tim, be our guest," my crew mates invited. I eased my way

Tim Neun

down the ladder. I had on my regular work clothes but no special protective gear. I was young. I was bigger than the baby. What could happen? The cat was frantic with fear and racing around the hole trying to escape my grip. Finally, I got it by the nape of its neck. It slashed the shit out of my pants, legs, coat sleeves then completely unprotected arms. The thing was fighting wildly, but I was able to climb up a couple of steps. With everything I had, tossed it out of the hole. It landed on the lip of the hole, caught the edge, and crawled out. This gave the other guys an extra second to jump out of its way. They scattered as it darted wildly around the area. The mom dashed over, knocked one guys on his ass, took a couple of nasty swipes at another, and then grabbed her cub by the neck and took off. All of this happened in under a nanosecond. Fucking thing was fast!

Slowly I pulled myself together and climbed up the ladder. I assessed my injuries as blood welled in all my slashes. By the time I got to the top of the ladder, I was bleeding profusely from my arms, legs, and face. The guys helped me up to the truck where there was a puny first aid kit. They wrapped me in gauze and bandages, loaded me onto a seat, and Dave drove me down off the mountain. Dave radioed ahead to tell Brenda, the work site nurse, to meet us in the first aid room in the main lodge.

Brenda was there waiting for us and when she saw me asked, "What the fuck happened to you!" As she cleaned up my wounds

Zig Zag

and checked to see how many needed stitches, Bob Meriwether, the building superintendent, wandered in, unprepared. "Jezus, fucking Christ, what the fuck happened to you?" Dave was retelling the story when Brenda broke in and told them I needed more attention than hers. She decided I needed to go to the doctor in Zig Zag. He had a clinic in a little town down the mountain. "Luckily the injuries on his face are superficial but there are some gashes on his arm and legs that will require stitches."

Bob pulled his car up, loaded me and Dave into the back seat and headed to Zig Zag. Zig Zag is a cool little village on the way to Mt. Hood. I think it is a great name, so I am going to say it as many times as I want: Zig Zag, Zig Zag, Zig Zag.

After only a couple of miles on the road, Dave noticed that some of my deeper cuts were dribbling blood on Bob's backseat. Bob got on his radio and found a state cop close by. We hooked up with him and he led us to the wonderfully named village of Zig Zag with flashing lights and the annoying siren blaring.

Forty-seven stitches later, I looked like a baby cougar had attacked me. Add antibiotics and some strong pain killers and I was ready for a rest from work and rescuing baby cougars. Bob drove us back to the cabin and I crashed for a couple of days.

CHAPTER 17

I recover,
I don't get to kill Marv

Dave replaced me on the crew during my cougar mauling recovery and I spent the time sleeping and eating and not thinking about anything. On the afternoon of my second day of recovery, Dave rushed into the cabin and blurted out, "Marv's DEAD!"

"Yeah right," I thought. Too good to be true. Sure, I had almost killed the fucker myself but fortunately, for me, the bail did not budge that day. "We better pour ourselves a glass of your dad's scotch and I'll tell you how it happened." I started to listen up and believe his news.

"Marv told us the bail was fixed," Dave said. "The first load worked fine but with every load after that it became more of a challenge to make it work. On the fifth load we could not open it and Marv immediately went into his regular rage. He was screaming and blaming us for breaking it again.

"He put his head under the bail and was reaching around under the bucket with his arm and yelling at the crew, 'Open the fucking bail!' The guy next to me screamed at Marv, 'Get the fuck out of the way because I'm going to open the bucket.' Marv was flipping the guy off. The guy operating the bail turned to me and shrugged, then he reefed on the bail. Unfortunately for Marv, it opened that time, struck Marv's head, and trapped him. The concrete dumped into the hole. The chopper lifted a few feet as the weight of the concrete was released. Marv was not moving, and his body hung from the bucket. For a moment we were all kind of paralyzed, staring at Marv, hanging there. Then we started frantically signaling the pilot to drop back down. The helicopter slowly lowered and one of the guys opened the bail. Marv's body slumped to the ground. The crew carried his body up to the truck and they drove him down the mountain to Brenda, but he was dead. Can you believe it?"

The rest of the summer went smoothly without Marv. There was no mourning among the crew, but we were a little subdued. The bail got fixed right, even though they had to call in mechanics to work over a Sunday. We watched out for each other and felt confidence in our crew teams.

After Marv's death, every tower was lifted into place and got bolted down smoothly, without a single glitch. All the cables were strung and spliced. Crews started attaching the chairs. The lodge was nearing completion. A new ski area was almost ready to open. It would be the biggest one on the mountain and it had great terrain. I looked forward to skiing The Meadows and checking out what I had helped build. Sure, I had scars from the baby cougar attack, but I had not killed anyone.

I said my goodbyes to Dave and the rest of the grunts, thinking I would never see any of them again. Then I headed off to college at the University of Oregon in Eugene.

LIFTING TOWER SECTION

EAR TO EAR

Chapter 18

A claustrophobic elevator ride to olfactory hell while blazing on LSD

I wandered down to the University of Oregon to begin my college career in September of 1967. I found my dorm, moved in and began attending classes the next day. My major: art/ceramics. My folks were thrilled! There was no discussion of money for college; they just took care of everything. All I had to do was show up. And I did not think about the gift at all. Talk about a privileged white kid!

My roommate was a guy named Murf, short for Murphy. He was a dedicated stoner and experimented with psychedelics. Murf showed me how to appreciate being high on weed. Going to classes and throwing pots while stoned made college far more enjoyable. I admit I was intimidated by college, but my fears diminished with my level of stonedness.

On the weekends Murf, myself and several other guys living in the same dorm took LSD. These young men were just as dedicated to their college careers as me. Maniacal laughter for eight or ten hours was the norm. Not a lot of studying was accomplished. Our jaws ached for days which we took as a sign of a great trip. Fortunately, nobody had a bum trip or freaked out.

We dropped some blotter acid one Saturday morning and decided a drive to the coast would keep us focused and occupied. Five of us jammed into my VW beetle and headed west from Eugene to the Oregon coast and then north on Hwy 101 to the major tourist attraction, The Sea Lion Caves. None of us had ever visited the caves and only had a vague idea what it was. Two hours later we were floating north along the ocean on the very curvy Highway 101 and, there it was, The Sea Lion Caves. It looked like a little gift shop. Once inside we saw that is exactly what is was. However, for a small fee, we could join the crowds and descend in an elevator to a huge cavern which opened to the Pacific Ocean. There we could commune with Stellar and California sea lions. This huge cavern was one of the few locations along the entire Pacific coast that the sea lions used as a birthing ground and swell hangout.

The cavern was accessed via an elevator that was finished in 1961. Before that everyone had to walk a series of wooden steps down to the viewing area. The elevator was much faster. About twenty-five people fit into the elevator that would take us down to a large viewing platform. We were thoroughly blazing away by then but able to purchase tickets without arousing too much attention. We blindly followed some kids and probably their parents to the elevator. We all jammed into it and watched the door close in front of us. This immediately set us on edge.

The proximity to a bunch of *straights* was unnerving. If they knew how stoned we were, how our current world was so much more heightened on all levels, than theirs, well who the fuck knows what they would do to us. We looked with glazed eyes at each other and collectively thought MAINTAIN, MAINTAIN, MAINTAIN!!!

I bet those folks could hear our thoughts because they started to look at us and tried to back away but there was no space in the elevator to back away into. We were all trapped together on this earthbound spaceship, which to us, was now free-falling down to lord knows where. We, the acid crazed, collectively knew (we just knew) that the straights had begun to realize something was amiss. The elevator ride down, in real time, was at most fifteen seconds, but by the time it stopped, those of us who were by now hallucinating wildly, were certain they would either turn on us or morph into grotesque aliens and rip us to shreds in a vibrant colorful display of a full-on psychedelic induced rampage.

Hours later, the elevator stopped at what turned out to be the third level of hell. The doors slowly and dramatically began to open. We were thrust into a world of sound no acid taker had ever experienced. This sound was the deafening roar of what had to be millions of sea lions, all barking at once. One half nanosecond later, while still attempting to grasp this cacophony, a solid wall of stink slammed into us. It engulfed us. It was an olfactory overload beyond comprehension. It was so strong it was visible to us.

The stink of more than a billion sea lions' shit was indescribable. Match that smell with the cacophony of sea lion barking and remember this is all being enhanced by the blotter acid. Due to our perfect timing, we were at a full LSD peak experience at that very moment. The smell of billions of pounds of sea lion shit and the barking noise was a perfect set up for a bum trip. This set us on our heels, so naturally, with drug induced thinking, we panicked. With wild eyes and no regard for the safety of others, we pushed the kids and adults out of the elevator, leapt back on, and huddled at the back.

SEA LION CAVE

From outside of the elevator the kids and parents turned and stared at us. We were paralyzed and gasping for breath. Our very lives were on the line. I crawled to the front of the elevator and began bashing the up button over and over. Slowly, ever so slowly, the elevator doors began to close. When the doors sealed shut with an ominous rush of air, we realized we were truly trapped. The reality of a complete LSD freak-out was upon us. At last the elevator began to rise from the gates of this olfactory/auditory hell on earth.

What seemed like hours later, the doors began to slowly open. All of us tried to exit simultaneously. The sight of us crawling over each other to escape our personal hell must have been quite startling. Imagine five, wild eyed, loudly gagging young men surging out of the elevator. Some of us were crying. We were so thankful to see freedom. When we got our first whiff of fresh air we began laughing hysterically. It was an image that naturally confused the patrons and they collectively backed away from the elevator doors and us.

We ran through the lobby/gift shop not bothering to purchase any swell trinkets to help us remember our adventure. We bolted for the car shouting, "We're alive! We made it out alive!" Now, whenever I drive past The Sea Lion Caves, a grand smile scrolls across my face as the memory, in vivid LSD color, flashes across my mind.

Tim Neun

Did I gain some sort of all-knowing wisdom after taking LSD? Did it give me some insight into the stupidity of being drafted to go thousands of miles away to another country to kill people because my country was into it? This was beyond nuts. I already felt that way. What if leaders were required to take psychedelics? Would they gain empathy? Would they see inside themselves and be horrified? Would anything change? Would they lose the all-consuming drive to attain power?

I should note that now (fifty-three years later) when I pass the Sea Lion Caves, my wife is usually with me and I regale her with the tale. She just loves hearing that story over and over again. "Oh, Tim please tell me the LSD/Sea Lion Caves story again, or, better yet, let me tell you!" She says with dripping sarcasm.

CHAPTER 19

Dr. Midnite to the rescue

Thirty days into my promising college career I got a call from Dave Gast. Remember Dave? We had just spent the summer together working as grunts on the lift crew at Mt. Hood Meadows.

He asked, "Hey, you want a job at Crystal Mountain on the Pro-Patrol and Avalanche crew?"

In less than twenty-nine minutes, my car was packed, and I was on my way north to Crystal. I told Murf where I was going and he was dumbfounded. Even stoned to the gills, he grasped the big picture better than I did. "What about your student deferment? You're gonna' end up getting drafted and get shipped off to Vietnam!"

I explained to him that in my heart I was a ski bum and this opportunity at Crystal was a dream come true. That was all that mattered at that moment. Being eighteen was great! My insight was instantaneous but not long sighted.

"Well take care and have a great time," Murf said. What a loyal friend.

At that moment I knew my student deferment was gone, "I'll deal with that later." That became one of my life mantras along with, "If there is a job worth doing, it's worth doing tomorrow."

I arrived at Crystal late that afternoon and got settled into the Pro-Patrol dorm. I called my folks and told them where I was and what was going on. My confession was greeted with their stunned realization that their child was, as they had suspected for quite some time, an idiot. I did not have the vaguest idea how much they had invested in my college tuition, clothes, books, and a year of dorm rent. A typical privileged white kid's complete lack of concern.

Jack, my dad, was a whiz with numbers and prorated the entire sum into the exact amount they had spent, per day, on my brief college career.

I heard a loud thump over the phone, "What was that?" I asked. Kay, my mom, nonchalantly remarked, "Oh that was just the sound of your father collapsing onto the kitchen floor." More thumping. "You hear that Tim? Now he's banging his forehead on the side of the stove."

There was silence for about ten seconds, then we started the conversation again. They asked, "What does work on the Pro-Patrol and Avalanche crew entail?" Fortunately, Dave had explained the duties a few minutes earlier because I had not asked before or after accepting the job.

"Well," I began gently, "on the avalanche crew we get to put forty or fifty pounds of high explosives in our rucksacks." Another loud thump. "Just your mom, her knees gave out and she dropped to the floor and is now sobbing."

"Then we get to hike up some steep mountain ridge-line which drops off precipitously on both sides to certain death if you slip." Another thump. Silence. They were loving this.

"It gets even better because usually the wind is howling, and the visibility is near zero, so it's tough to even see the ridge we are hiking up." Another thump.

"Then we get to assemble two pound explosive charges and lob them over the side to trigger avalanches!"

I heard my dad, "Kay, just stay on the floor."

"Think of the Pro-Patrol as first responders. We ski to the injured person on the mountain, perform any first aid needed, then strap them into an Akia (a sled) and take them down to the first aid room. The volunteer patrol, the Jolly Vollies, meet us there and assess the situation. We get the person into a bed and help the Jolly Vollies if they need us."

The Jolly Vollies were great. They knew their shit. They studied first aid and there was usually a volunteer doctor or nurse on duty. It was great to hand off someone injured to a person who was qualified. All the Jolly Vollies got free skiing for volunteering.

"Well that sounds nice" my mom says.

"Yeah, that part is pretty boring. I get all my first aid training the day after tomorrow."

My folks were more adventurous than most. They moved from Detroit to Seattle and learned to ski when they were in their forties. They got to be pretty damn good skiers. They learned to ski using shitty leather boots, long shitty skis, miserable non-waterproof clothes in the rainy Northwest. They also had shitty bindings, shitty goggles that fogged up the moment you put them on and shitty water-absorbing gloves. The lifts were excruciatingly slow. Get the picture? It is amazing anybody put up with such lousy equipment for a few turns. My parents took me with them and put me in the care of a ski instructor while they skied. I was about eight when I started. Apparently, from what my brother Mike says, I hated skiing.

Looking back, I wonder if it was some sort of torture my folks enjoyed putting me through. I was an accident, their accident, but somehow, I was to blame. Little did they know, at the time, they had created an expensive monster, who would cost them dearly in time, money, and heartache.

They signed me up for ski lessons at Ski Acres, a little ski area on Snoqualmie Pass which was about fifty miles from our house in Bellevue.

My group included eight rank beginners about my age. Our instructor showed up and he was an old guy. We didn't know twenty-five from sixty. He introduced himself as Leo and asked our names.

We all looked at him blankly. None of us had a clue what he was saying. His accent was so thick everything he said was unintelligible. He knew the problem and so he just smiled and waved his arm, "Follow me." That we understood.

We wandered around on the flats until we could kind of walk with the giant slabs (skis) strapped to our feet. Occasionally he would turn, look at us laughing and say, "Ahh be darned." I learned to ski following Leo and doing what he did.

We followed him everywhere even though we never understood a word he said except, "Ahh be darned," and his wonderful laugh. Flat stuff, steep stuff, moguls, headwalls, it made no difference. Our spatial awareness at eight years old may have reached the tips of our skis. We just followed Leo. He made sure we had fun. Leo Scheiblehner taught me to ski.

So, thanks, Mom and Dad, for making me take ski lessons. It turned out good for me. Sorry about all the money and heartache I cost you.

Back to Crystal Mountain. Dave picked me up the next morning and we headed for the day lodge. The first aid room had a changing room and lockers to stash our equipment.

We grabbed our skis and rucksacks, walked to the main lift, and headed to the top of the mountain to meet the other guys and begin avalanche training. What a great day: the first day of my life as a ski bum!

Dave and I met the rest of the crew having a cup of coffee at the summit restaurant. We walked in and I was introduced to everyone. They welcomed me warmly.

I was putting cream and sugar into my coffee with my back to the door when it opened and I heard a familiar, "Ahh be darned."

What the fuck? Sure as shit, it was Leo, my old ski instructor from Ski Acres. He was the head of the avalanche crew! I walked over, shook his hand, and told him, "I know you!" He looked at me with a puzzled smile. "You taught me to ski at Ski Acres ten years ago!"

His eyes lit up. He didn't remember me specifically, I'm sure, but he laughed and said, "Ahh be darned." His accent had not diminished

LEO SCHEIBLEHNER

a bit. "Now you're really going to learn how to ski." He seemed happy to have me there. He had a second chance to teach me.

Little did I know how right he was.

While we finished coffee, Leo explained, well who knows what the hell he said. At the end of his speech, he turned and headed out the door. We all got up and followed him back down to the patrol hut. He gave each of us ten pounds of HDP explosive which we gently placed into our rucksacks. This was just a practice day. Leo took the yellow primer cord and Dave was given the fuse to carry. We all carried igniter's.

We skied down to the saddle above one of the ski runs, Lucky Shot, and climbed to the top of the Silver Queen. I had never skied Crystal, so I was completely unfamiliar with the territory. The wind was blowing about sixty mph and it was snowing. Visibility was about thirty feet. They told me that from the top of Queen, Mt. Rainier is about twenty miles away, and, on a nice day, it is very impressive. Mt. Rainier is the tallest mountain in the cascades. It is 14,410 feet above sea level and is easily the most massive mountain in the Cascade range. No stunning view of Mt. Rainier today.

We reached the top and it dawned on me, my 215-centimeter Head downhill skies might not be suitable for this job. They were too long and too heavy. Jack Nagel owned the ski shop in the lodge and so right after work I strolled in and bought a pair of pimp sticks. 205 cm. Rossignol Stratos. Jack let me mount the bindings, tune, and wax them in his shop.

He and his daughters, Judy and Kathy, were working on their skis in the shop. Judy and Kathy were both on the US Olympic ski team. At that moment I fell deeply in love with them both. They never noticed me. That Neun magic workin' it's spell.

Back to the top of the Queen. Leo grabbed two, two-pound cylinders of HDP, cut a piece of primer cord, ran it through each cylinder and tied some sort of knot. He measured the fuse with his hand (thirty seconds worth), taped it to the primer cord, and slid the igniter on.

He carefully explained every step because our lives depended on properly assembling each charge. I did not understand a fucking word he said. His accent was too thick and the howl of the wind was too loud. I kept my eyes open.

Thump, my mom hitting the kitchen floor again.

Leo pulled the igniter, held the charge to his ear for a few moments to make sure the fuse was burning then gently lobbed it over the cornice and into the chute. He started counting in German: eins, zwei, drei, vier, funf. When he hit twenty-seven seconds the charge went off with a big thump (my mom again?). The charge dropped into two feet of snow so the sound of it exploding was muffled. You got it, thump. The chute pulled out, avalanche! Cool! We all watched it rage down the mountain as we were standing on the edge of the cornice to get the best view.

"Ahh be darned," Leo said from about ten feet back. He was not excited by the explosion or slide, he was relieved because the cornice did not shear off, taking us with it. Success!

Leo pointed to me and said, again, lord knows what. I gathered he wanted me to try assembling a charge and lob it over the side. I had been watching Leo intently. I nervously assembled the charge mimicking Leo's moves. I was too nervous to hold the charge to my ear after pulling the igniter. I merely swept it past my ear and awkwardly tossed it. It did not go over the edge of the cornice. It dropped about six feet in front of the crew. Leo started moving back the moment the charge landed. Then we stopped staring at the charge and followed Leo. After thirty seconds there was a very loud explosion, no gentle thump and the cornice held its ground.

We heard Leo trying to say, "Ahh be darned," but he could not get it out as he was doubled over, laughing.

We continued to assemble charges, skied down to the next chute and lob them in. We got used to pulling the igniter and making damn sure the fuse was lit by holding it to our ear.

Mom, Dad, as skiers, if you had been there in that storm, on that ridge, lobbing explosives, you would have loved it.

Crystal is a great mountain. It is made up of four separate peaks which each have big, steep bowls. There are countless near vertical chutes and headwalls galore. The only thing it lacks is true powder snow. It never gets cold enough for honest powder.

The ski areas on the west side of the Cascades receive storms mostly from the west straight off the Pacific Ocean. These storms deliver huge amounts of snow, but the temperatures are usually too close to freezing, too warm for real powder snow. What Crystal receives is wet glop and high winds. These are superb conditions for massive slides. The slopes are steep, and the snow can build and build then pull out in huge slides. I saw one fracture line that was six feet tall. It was made of heavy snow and had a swell, heavily crusted, windblown surface. The steeper the slope, the easier it is to ski. The medium and flat pitched slopes, with that kind of snow condition, are scary.

Years later I occasionally experienced the same kind of conditions at Sun Valley's ski area, Mt. Baldy. Nearly everybody freaked. Most stayed on the groomers. The bowls and south slopes were, for those of us from the Northwest, a bonanza. The skiers from the Northwest went right to the uncluttered bowls and chutes choked with crud, a dream come true. We had run after run of untracked bat guano.

I patrolled the bat guano choked chutes and slide paths all over Crystal. The crew included one woman, Hurly Johnson. She was a strong, stylish skier and a good friend. Hurly was the first woman on the pro-patrol and avalanche crew at Crystal. It was tough being the first woman on the crew. Sure, lots of women were on the mountain, but they were there for recreation not work. She became respected for her hard work and willingness to deal with frightened injured skiers. When we knew the injury was likely to be serious, we tried to get Hurly to go. Some of the avalanche crew were uncomfortable dealing with injured skiers on the mountain. I didn't mind heading out for rescues, especially with Hurly.

My last name is Neun, which is pronounced "noon." Since I often volunteered to go on rescues with Hurly, I got the nickname Dr. Midnite. As a joke, the crew made an official name tag for me: Dr. Midnite, right there in red and white with the ski patrol insignia. It was official. Everyone now called me Dr. Midnite instead of Tim or Noon, or Nooner.

At the fiftieth reunion of the Pro-Patrol and Avalanche crew members, Hurly reminded me of a story that still pissed her off. First, Hurly was twenty-three the first year we worked on the mountain together. She was an experienced skier and had extensive emergency response training. When we went on a call, she was in charge. I was only eighteen that first winter and I had one day of basic first aid training.

On the day of this story, we were called to a spot on the beginner section of the mountain to evacuate some wreck. The woman had an injured leg, possibly broken. Hurly evaluated her injury and stabilized her leg. Then we lifted her into the Akia, picked up her gear, and got her down the mountain as quickly as possible.

We delivered her to the Jolly Vollies. Fortunately, they had a doctor and a nurse on that shift, and we were able to hand her over to their care. We moved her into a bed and went upstairs to the cafeteria for a cup of coffee.

After our coffee break we went back down to the first aid room to see how she was doing. She had been given pain medication for her injury which turned out to be a simple fracture and she seemed much happier. Hurly asked how she was doing. She stared at me with dreamy eyes, ignoring Hurly, and said, "Much better, Dr. Midnite. Thanks for helping me. I am so glad they have a doctor who can ski. You are soooo young to be a doctor."

Hurly turned to me and gave my name plate the evil eye. "He's not a doctor," she told the woman.

"Then why does his name tag say, Dr. Midnite?"

The Jolly Vollies in hearing range laughed and laughed while Hurly eventually gave in and touched the woman's shoulder, "It's his nickname."

When we got back to the top of the mountain to the patrol shack, the news of my new status had already reached the crew. I was greeted with, "Hey, It's Dr. Midnite!"

After that, the call went out to Dr. Midnite for every tiny scratch or hangnail. If there was a serious need on the mountain, Hurly was called in.

I spent two winters on the avalanche crew at Crystal Mountain. Those two years were a highlight of my life. I have fond memories, lasting friendships and, as Leo predicted, I really learned how to ski.

CHAPTER 20

The Dull Green Room

S it here, a guy in an unadorned army green uniform barked at me. "Fuck you," I thought and took a chair five seats away in the second row.

He glared at me. I bet he was thinking, "In an hour that civilian trouble-maker is all mine."

Another young dude in bell bottoms with long greasy hair stumbled into the dull green room. He stared around the green room with some weed induced confusion in his eyes and sat down as directed.

I looked around and saw that not only were the ceiling and walls painted a particularly dull green, but the floor was the same shade of green linoleum. The metal folding chairs were the same shade of green, the doors, the venetian blinds, all matched in color. The ceiling reflected a dull green light. It finally dawned on me: Army green.

The room gradually filled with silent young men my age. We did not talk to each other. I don't know what they were thinking, but I was clear and calm and ready to get this over with.

When most of the chairs were full, a different dull green uniformed guy barked at the first row of us silent civilians to, "Follow me." The front row shuffled behind him through one of the green doors. It closed behind them, while my row, the second row, sat staring silently at the closing door. The door slowly shut with a solid finality that made a few of the remaining guys sit up. "Hey, fuckers, we mean business," the door seemed to say.

Seven minutes later the same door opened, and a different uniformed guy growled, "Follow me," and walked through the door into the next room. The first group was gone, disappeared, perhaps out the second dull green door in the back of the room.

This room was amazing and not like anything I'd ever seen before. You guessed it, dull green. And there were flags everywhere. There was an American flag that completely covered one wall; I knew that flag. There were flags on flagpoles lining the perimeter of the room. I had no idea what they represented but guessed they were from different Army battalions or platoons.

There was large wooden desk with another uniformed army dude sitting behind it. The front of the desk was plastered some kind of official seal that matched the rest of the interior design. The man behind the desk was looking down at the paperwork on his desk and ignoring the bunch of us standing in front of him. His uniform was festooned with brightly colored and striped doodads. He had lots of patches on his sleeves and over his shoulders was draped fancy gold braid. He reminded me of a grown-up Eagle Scout. This dude must really be important! I wondered what the military spent on flags, stripy doodads, patches, gold braid and dull green paint.

There were two fat bright yellow lines painted on the floor stretching across the room. These two lines were the only marks on the floor and were impossible to miss.

Our uniformed guy ordered us to stand directly behind the first yellow line. Two of the guys in my group (say we call them Earl and Cletus), missed the mark. The uniformed guy stood nose to nose facing them and uttered,

"I did not ask you to stand on the line. I asked you to stand directly behind the line!"

They sheepishly looked down and saw the tips of their shoes were a quarter inch onto the yellow line. They both jumped back six inches. Wrong again, Earl and Cletus. Once again, the uniformed guy got right in their faces and in a more menacing and sinister voice growled, "Stand Directly Behind the Line!" It took Cletus and Earl another two attempts to get it right. Already everybody in the room sensed that those two were going to have a trying Army experience. I was thankful I was not going where they were going. These guys in dull green uniforms had this intimidation shit down pat. They must practice a lot! As soon as Earl and Cletus got correctly situated the fancy uniformed guy stood up.

He intoned, "Gentlemen, in order to join the armed forces of the United States, you must now STEP...UP...TO...BUT...NOT...ON... THE...NEXT...YELLOW...LINE." Towards the end of the order he spoke more and more slowly and loudly. His eyes were drilling through Earl and Cletus. He continued to give the two boneheads the evil eye as everyone in my group looked down at their shoes and stepped over the first yellow line, BUT...NOT...ON...THE... NEXT...YELLOW...LINE, except for me. I did not step up to the next yellow line.

The fancy uniform guy looked at me and asked, "Are you here to refuse induction?" He guessed correctly.

"Yes," I said, "I am here to refuse induction."

All the inductees' eyes were on me. I could read their minds, "Well, fuck me runnin', why didn't I think of that?"

Fancy uniform dude got the inductees' attention by ordering them to repeat after him an oath that made them part of the U.S. Army. "Congratulations, gentlemen, you are now members of the greatest fighting force in the world, the United States Army." They were officially drafted and off to boot camp.

Yet another dull green guy opened a different dull green door and ordered everyone in my group, except me, to follow him out.

The important guy slowly looked up from the important papers on his important desk and said to me nonchalantly, "You will be contacted within thirty days by the Federal Marshal's office. You are free to go." He motioned to the door where I had entered and looked down at his desk and papers again.

Goddamn right I am free to go, you dull green fuck. That's it? No lecture? No intimidation? No handcuffs?

CHAPTER 21

My life of crime comes to an end

I received a very official letter from the Oregon U.S. District Court about thirty days later. It informed me where and when to show up for my court date. I must admit I was a tad disappointed.

My dad called a lawyer friend and he gave us the name of another lawyer who had experience representing *conscientious objectors*.

I called him and we talked over my reason for refusing induction. I told him, "I just don't believe what the President, generals and chicken hawks are telling us. I'll be damned if I'm going to kill or get killed for their lies."

"So, let me get this straight," he said. "You are not some religious nut job nor are you claiming you cannot be part of any war due to your strict moral code." Ironically, killing was not against my strict moral code as I had already killed two people, which I did not mention. Silence. I could not think of one more thing to say.

Finally, my lawyer said, "Your reasoning is spot on and I'm with you one hundred percent but a federal judge, who answers to the president may, just may, be unsympathetic to your argument. I'll meet you in court. You cannot tell the judge what you just told me, or you will get two years in prison, guaranteed. Do your best to come up with a statement, a very short statement, under ten seconds. Use a few sincere words that do not tell the judge and the entire federal government to go fuck themselves."

I arrived in the hallway outside of the designated courtroom where my lawyer met me and introduced himself. "Well, did you come up with a statement?" he asked.

"Yes, it is short, concise and tells nobody to go fuck themselves."

He looked relieved but still not confident of my speaking skills. There was no time for a rehearsal, so we went right into the court to be on time.

My lawyer introduced me to the judge and uttered a few words about young men who have chosen to refuse induction into the armed forces.

After a few moments, the judge turned to me and asked, "Do you have anything to say?"

"Yes, your honor, I am sorry my actions are necessary," I said sincerely.

The judge and my lawyer looked at each other and shrugged in approval. They were both thinking, "Well he kept it under ten seconds, hell, he kept it under five! At least he didn't waste our time."

The judge completed his duties by intoning, "Six months at South Fork Camp and eighteen months probation at a job in the interest of the nation." Gavel down. "Next."

The court clerk said, "The Federal Marshall's office will contact you."

Back in the hallway I asked my lawyer, "What is a job in the interest of the nation?"

"Kids' home, hospital, highway crew, but find something, anything, as quick as you can because you only have thirty days when you get out of prison to find that job. If you do not have a job the first month out, they will throw you back in jail. Relax; they accept damn near anything; they don't have time to fuck with you."

My parents, Jack and Kay were afraid for me. They were disappointed that I had blown off college to become a ski bum. Now I was twenty years old and going to prison for *failure to submit to induction*. Not the trajectory they were hoping for.

They were genuinely frightened at the idea of me being in prison. We knew I would be going to a minimum-security work camp located somewhere in the Oregon Coast range. None of us had any idea what that meant. Most people imagined a prison with tall walls, cells, bars, mean guards, and meaner convicts.

My parents belonged to the Oswego Lake Country Club. They played golf. They played bridge with a large group of friends.

I am certain they heard, "Our son, Biff, is majoring in business at Yale." "Our daughter, Buffy, is in the pre-med program at Johns Hopkins."

"Our son, Tim, is a ski bum, but he is taking a gap year to go to prison because he refused induction into the army." How proud they must have been. Years later I asked my brother, Mike, what they thought of me. He told me, "Your stand made them reconsider much of their conservative opinions. They were proud of you." Maybe, but they could not brag at the country club like their friends.

They visited me at South Fork several times as it was kind of on the way to the beach house in Salishan. They were relieved to see I was not locked up in an ordinary prison. I wish I could have overheard how they handled the Biff and Buffy conversations on the golf course and around the bridge table. Thank God they did not know about the rape or murders.

CHAPTER 22

Prison, A Highpoint in Life

I was right to be afraid even though South Fork Work Camp was not an ordinary prison. It was a dangerous place for a naïve twenty-year-old ski bum.

I arrived in camp on a Friday afternoon in November. On Monday, I would start planting trees. I had the weekend to get used to my new digs. There were about fifty of us in the camp. We were fed in the dining room which was locked between meals. There was ample simple food prepared by inmates. Some of the older cons could not keep up planting trees on the steep and rugged terrain so they cooked instead.

We were issued denim shirts and pants, work boots, shoes, and heavy duty rain gear so we could work outdoors during the Oregon winter. They gave us a hoedad and a large canvas bag with a shoulder strap. There was a craft shop where one could sharpen a hoedad.

The wash was done by another group of older inmates. We generated a lot of incredibly filthy laundry by working in the woods during a wet winter. We put our clothes into the magic basket and our cleaned and folded clothes would appear on our bunks the next day.

My first night was hell. Cho Mo and Walkin' Death raped me. They invited me out for a smoke and overpowered me. I did not tell anyone, but, before the night was over, every inmate knew what had happened.

I found out later that the inmates, the guards and even the warden hated Walkin' Death and Cho Mo because they were child molesters. I learned that a child molester was the lowest of the low. No child molester is safe in prison. The reputation of a child molester is passed along from inmate to inmate. They are viewed with disgust. Inmates plot to murder them if the chance presents itself. Each one must keep his wits about him or be snuffed during his stay. If you kill a child molester, your cred is established, forever. You will do easy time. This is what I learned after my rape.

South Fork Work Camp was much better than a regular prison. A prison is supposed to keep convicts secure behind tall walls and electrified razor wire. There were no tall walls or razor wire at South Fork Camp. If you wanted, you could just walk away. However, you would automatically get five years tacked onto your sentence if you sauntered away.

We had pleasant little hand-routed Forest Service wood signs posted around the edges of the camp. Each sign was about a foot and a half tall and noted the "Camp Limit." The signs appeared to be randomly spaced around the perimeter of the camp. Inmates were expected to have the ability to resist walking away. It was a test.

Each year one or two guys would leave anyway. A guy nicknamed Booger walked away while I was there. His story was about the saddest thing I heard there. He was a nice guy but not that sharp. He was in for stealing food. His escape was not planned. He just starting walking down the gravel road towards the highway. After five miles, he was tired and hungry. Eventually it dawned on him he had no place to go. Booger wanted to come back to South Fork. When he saw one of the guards coming to work, he recognized the man and waved him down. Not only did he get a ride back to the camp, he got five years tacked onto his sentence and was sent back to the main penitentiary in Salem, Oregon, the next day. Bummer. He cried all night before he left.

South Fork Camp was an old Forest Service facility. Since there was not much forest left, they abandoned the work camp. The Department of Corrections claimed it and turned into a work camp for short timers. It served as a kind of halfway house for non-violent inmates and those who were nearing the end of their sentences.

South Fork Camp was unusually peaceful, for a prison. The regular inmates, who were on their way out, were on their best behavior. If they fucked up, they would be sent back to the main prison in Salem. They had been to the real joint and they did not want to go back. This was the good life, for prison. Steady hard work, three squares, a roof over their head, and some camaraderie. Many of these inmates had never known such comforts, even on the outside.

I was in prison prior to the massive influx of drug related criminals. When I was at South Fork, the inmates represented a more interesting cross section of the criminal mind. Bank robbers, murderers, burglars, thieves, armed robbers, you know, regular guys. These were guys who were trying to get money the easy way and got caught. Many of them were like the guys I met in Outward Bound. They did not have a lot of choices, little education, families who could not help them, and they did not go to Outward Bound. Except for Cho Mo and Walkin' Death who were simply just a couple of disgusting turds.

Many were smart and witty. The tales they told were fascinating. They laughed about how poorly planned their criminal escapades were. Usually an unexpected opportunity presented itself and they simply acted without forethought. They were drunk and drove by a house with an open window. It was three a.m. Well, shall we take a quick look inside? Sure!

Driving by a bank with a gun in the glove box and only eleven dollars in cash in his pocket. Time to restock. Mostly they did this shit on a whim and had no thought for the consequences. Surprisingly nice guys except for the guns and crime part.

I mean, I had killed two people so who was I to judge? I was a nice guy except for the murdering part. I had not thought about the consequences. I was just trying to get by day to day.

We were all resigned to being in prison and doing our time. They were thinking they needed to plan future crimes more carefully. I asked, "What about rehabilitation? What about going straight?"

Howls of laughter. "Any suggestions? We can't get jobs. We're felons just released from prison. Nobody will hire us. Besides, we don't know how to do anything. Anyway, getting a job sounds like work."

Back then there were no opportunities offered in prison to take a class or learn a trade. They asked me about my past jobs. When they heard about the avalanche crew, their only interest was to learn how to assemble the explosive charges. They were all ears when the topic of blowing shit up was discussed. I am proud to have instructed several them how to handle explosives safely.

During the summer, the inmates were sent to fight fires all over the state. In the winter, the inmates planted trees in the Tillamook Burn. The fire burned over 350,000 acres of old growth forest from 1933 to 1951. What was left was logged and after the second growth reached maturity it was logged again. We planted in the clear cuts left over from extensive logging. It was ugly territory, just stumps and torn up hills as far as the eye could see. With no trees the views were stunningly barren.

Monday morning I got a lesson in how to use a hoedad, follow the line, and put a foot-high fir tree seedling with foot long roots into the ground with one stroke so that it would survive. Planting trees requires climbing steep hillsides in a line and planting trees every fifteen feet. We climbed up and down the steep hills and carried one hundred seedlings in a heavy canvas bag slung over our shoulder. You climbed, stopped, drove your hoedad into the ground, hoping you did not hit rock, which you always did, pulled it toward you, pushed it away, pulled to toward you, placed the little tree with long roots into the hole made by the hoedad and used it to push soil in place around the seedling. Then you slogged up the line another fifteen

Hoedad

or so feet and did it again. One hundred fifty times in the morning and 150 times after lunch. My youth, mountaineering experience, and ski work the last two years were helpful. I was in good shape for this job. It was still a challenge and very hard work.

If you saw us in our crummy on the highway or planting trees in the woods, you would not know we were convicts. There was no visible indication. No *inmate* bullshit on the back of our shirts. We wore denim.

Denim shirts, denim pants, denim coats. Our work boots were good rubber boots. The vehicles that schlepped us to the woods and back were nondescript. They were called *crummys* and were red Chevy's. They were trucks that could seat up to ten guys. This anonymity gave the short timers a taste of freedom.

We planted trees during the week and had the weekends off. There was little energy for fighting or hassling others. All of us, including me wanted out of prison and we did not want to fuck with anyone. Except for Cho Mo and Walkin' Death.

The guards did not go out with the work crews and they did not carry guns in the camp. Fatigue is a good way to keep a minimum-security prison peaceful. There was not much energy left for escape after a day of planting trees. The inmates whose sentences were winding down were on their best behavior. The threat of being sent back to the main joint in Salem was a good incentive to stay cool.

Tim Neun

The tree planting bosses were civilians; they didn't pack a gun either. If you wanted to walk away while working, you could. It was not part of their job to stop you. Even the guys who walked away did not escape. There just wasn't any place to go. Nobody really escaped; those who attempted were eventually picked up and sent back to the joint with more time tacked onto their sentences.

I was in for refusing induction into the armed forces. I did not claim to be a conscientious objector. I was aware of the irony of my situation. On one hand I was in prison for refusing to take part in the Vietnam War, a murderous enterprise; on the other hand I had already murdered two people.

One of the other inmates was a conscientious objector. He used the religious nutcase excuse. "God told me I shall not kill." I think he was faking it because he never talked about any other religious beliefs and was as profane as the rest of us, but he had to stick to his story, and he did. He was also an obnoxious fucker. If there is a God, he is screwed.

I heard other conscientious objectors who claimed killing was against their moral code. They believed, along with me, our 'leaders' President Johnson, Senators, Congressmen as well as military pawns, like McNamara, were lying through their asses. They would sacrifice the lives of over 282,000 American and Allied soldiers, 444,000 North Vietnamese combatants and over 627,000 Vietnamese citizens. I am an atheist, but in this case I hope those responsible for Vietnam rot in Hell.

On my first day, when the tree planting crew arrived at the day's site, we lined up across the area to be planted. We stood about ten yards from each other.

Our crew boss was a forest service employee. He taught us how to use the tools and insured we planted the trees properly, so they had a chance to grow. His name was Larry Long. Larry was a short chubby gregarious guy with a booming laugh. We lucked out with him. His nickname was Larry-Long-Dong for obvious reasons. I was a kid and his was the first big cock I had ever seen. When you gotta pee in the woods you just stop, get it out, turn away from the other guys and whiz. Let us just say his pecker was hard not to notice.

Larry drove the crummy from South Fork Camp to the area to be planted and back. Before we climbed out of the crummy, he always said, "If you want to leave, all you have to do is walk away, don't hurt me, especially me, or anybody else." We mocked him every morning by joining in with the *Larry-Long-Dong Pledge*. He cracked up every time.

Larry always started out on the left and set a pace appropriate for the terrain. The rest of us spread out diagonally across the slope and started planting. On my first day, one of the guys who had raped me, Cho Mo, was working with the crew farther down the line. He was in the far-right position and I was somewhere near the middle. We always planted old clear cuts which are crisscrossed with numerous logging roads. Prison crews got the contracts for the steepest, rockiest, least fertile acreage. There was a private tree-planting outfit called the Hoedads who got the best contracts. The prison crews were left with the crap ground the Hoedads refused to bid on.

This day was a miserable wet, dark, cloudy one. It was a normal Oregon winter day. Larry stopped the crummy on an old logging road siding. We were planting starting at the road in a section with very steep hills. All the side cuts down to the next road were nearly drop-offs and as much as two hundred feet deep. These side cuts were strewn with large boulders the size of cars. This was extraordinarily terrible terrain, even for us. Everyone was grumbling. We could not see more than a couple of guys on the line it was so dark and rainy. We all looked the same, green rain pants, green raincoat, and a green rain hat. Tough to tell who was who out there.

I had not planned to take my revenge out on Cho Mo so soon, but the opportunity presented itself. I found a rhythm and could work a bit faster than the line. I slowly passed guys on my right until I was in position planting next to Cho Mo.

Cho Mo never noticed me moving closer to him. Larry was on my left over a slight rise, out of sight. The rest of the line was just barely visible, a line of moving shadows.

Cho Mo was working along the edge and approached a particularly steep and rocky road cut. I kept planting trees and intentionally fell behind him a few yards until he reached the biggest drop off. Then I came up behind him and I nailed him with a strong swing to the side of his head with my hoedad.

Cho Mo toppled over the edge and took a nasty route to the bottom. His limp body ricocheted off the boulders, finally coming to rest in the ditch of the road below. He did not move; he was probably dead after I hit him, if not, he sure the fuck was by the time he got to the bottom.

I worked my way to the left now, past Mumbles and Spaz, and back to the center of the line. Larry did not notice a thing. If the other guys did, they did not show it in any way. They were minding their own business.

We got back to the crummy at the end of the day and Larry took a headcount. One short, Cho Mo. This did not faze Larry a bit. He asked if anybody knew where Cho Mo might be. Mumbles and Spaz said, "We saw him walk away towards the highway."

"Uh huh."

Larry shrugged his shoulders and hopped into the crummy.

I was surprised to hear this. Were Mumbles and Spaz trying to cover for me? Well, they knew that Cho Mo had raped me. Everyone did. Normally it was deathly quiet on the ride back because after a long day of climbing up and down the steep slopes everybody was beat, but today there was a lot of chatter about Cho Mo and where he might be.

Tim Neun

When we got back to camp, Larry went straight to the warden to let him know Cho Mo was missing. There was no drama. They talked for a few minutes and chuckled from time to time. We went off to our cabins to change out of our work clothes and dry off.

By the time we were all changed and on our way to the dining hall, a couple of unmarked police cars and one state police car showed up. The cops got out and we could see them talking to Larry and the warden. Suddenly another state cop car came ripping into the camp. The cop jumped out of his car talking and gesturing excitedly. Then all the cops got into their cars and high tailed it out of the camp, lights flashing and sirens blaring.

The news about Cho Mo walking off spread to everyone in the camp before dinner. The cons were more interested than the guards. Cho Mo was gone. The guards didn't give a shit.

The warden talked to all of us on Larry's crew. Mumbles and Spaz repeated they saw Cho Mo walk away towards the highway and the rest of the crew said they had no idea what happened; if they did, they kept their mouths shut. They told the warden the obvious, "It was so dark and wet out there, we could barely see where we were going."

Even though Larry always said, "If you want to leave, just walk away," I could hardly believe the lack of drama after Larry told the warden and guards. This is when I started hearing how much everyone hated Cho Mo and Walkin' Death.

It was now dark and cold. The two unmarked cars and one state cop car leisurely rolled back into camp. We could see all of them get out of their cars and stroll into the warden's office. Twenty minutes later they moseyed off.

I think Mumbles and Spaz were aware of what had happened. They were short timers and, hopefully, would like to avoid any attention. Plus, I think they thought he had it coming. There is honor among thieves. I can personally tell you it is true.

We learned later that evening, from one of the guards, that Cho Mo apparently lost his footing a fell down a steep road cut. "He must have slammed his head on one of the rocks on his way down because it was completely bashed in on one side. A lot of broken bones," the guard said.

I decided to act quickly, so that night immediately after dinner, I went to the craft shop. I sharpened my hoedad. No one else was there, probably because none of them cared to sharpen their hoedads. It was not my main goal either. While I was in there, I took a small file and went off to one of the toilets.

Once in the toilet, I took out the spoon I had pinched from the dining hall and started to sharpen one side. It doesn't take long to make a sharp edge. I had to leave the toilet before I was finished, but I was able to get up during the night and finish my work. That spoon would never hold soup again.

The next day, I approached Walkin' Death, my other attacker, and told him I needed to talk to him. He knew that if I told the guards what he and Cho Mo had done to me, his ass was cooked. He looked suspicious but said, "OK."

"Meet me behind the craft shop by the wood pile at midnight."

We planted trees all day. Walkin' Death was on my crew that day. He had lost his accomplice and only friend. He looked haggard and gray. I am sure he had started to realize what the consequences of his abuse of me might be.

I came down just before midnight and hid behind the stacked firewood. It seemed prudent to not trust this motherfucker. Before Walkin' Death showed up another con, Thumbs, appeared and wandered around aimlessly. Thumbs was a name he earned because his got cut off in some lumber mill. Thumbs never saw me and eventually left. Walkin' Death showed up even later and I let him hang out for an hour and he finally gave up.

The next morning Walkin' Death sat down across from me at breakfast. "Missed you last night. How was your night?"

"It was crowded, WD, it was real crowded," I explained. "If you want to get this figured out, you better come to talk to me alone. Leave your fuck-for-brains buddy, Thumbs, out of this. This is between me and you. You told me to keep quiet and I have. You know that no one can find out, right?"

"Right." He was chastened. He looked like an old man who was cracking up. He couldn't do any more time in prison as a child molester. He and Cho Mo just were not built right.

"Meet me a two a.m. behind the craft shop by the wood pile, tonight."

"O.K."

The craft shop was built on a slope so the side not facing the camp, the side in the dark, was elevated about six feet off the ground and supported by six by six vertical posts with two by six cross members. It was a moonless night and I had been there, hiding under the crafts shop, for a couple of hours. By two a.m. my eyes had become accustomed to the dark.

Walkin' Death was too stupid to let his eyes adjust to the darkness. He was slow, touching the six by six's and two by six's to guide himself. He couldn't see shit. I could see everything, perfectly, from under the craft shop in the pitch black.

The moment Walkin' Death was directly in front of me, I reached out, grabbed his hair and pulled his head back into one of the 6x6"s with all my strength. I heard his skull crack. At the same moment, I reached around and slit his throat from ear to ear. His blood was copious. His blood was dark. Walkin' Death gurgled once and collapsed on the ground. I moved out from under the craft shop, put the razor-sharp spoon in his hand and whispered, "Hope it was worth dying for, you fucking piece of shit."

They found the bastard the next morning and shut the camp down. Turns out everybody

Tim Neun

185

really did hate him. The warden hated him, the guards hated him, and the rest of the cons hated him. Walkin' Death was the cause of a lot of trouble for the guards and warden. They all knew he had raped a number of inmates while he was at South Fork, they just couldn't prove it. The place was swarming with state police and prison officials from Salem for most of the day and they questioned every single inmate. All the cons said they were happy the fucker was dead and had no clue as to how it happened. We learned through the grapevine that the official cause of death was suicide. I did easy time.

LIKE I SAID, REGULAR GUYS

CHAPTER 23

Probation Hell in Sun Valley

My brother, Mike Neun, was the most talented comedian you've never heard of. In 1971 he and his partner, Brian Bressler, toured as "Mike and Brian, an act as exciting as its name" and were working the Ram Bar in Sun Valley, Idaho.

After one of their shows Mike was sitting at a table with a bunch of locals and somehow my story came up. Mike explained that I needed to find a job in "the interest of the nation." One of the guys at the table, Mark Ackerman, told Mike, "I like what your brother did. When he gets out of prison have him contact me. I can offer him a job at the Moritz Community Hospital in Sun Valley. I run the place." He gave Mike his card which he put in his pocket.

Mike rescued the card just as he was putting his pants into the washing machine and left me a message at South Fork. "Come to Sun Valley, I got you a job at the hospital!"

I was released from prison on a Friday and was in Ketchum by Sunday afternoon. Monday morning at 7:30 a.m., I was at the hospital and by 8:01 a.m. I was sitting across the desk from Mr. Ackerman.

I clearly remember enthusiastically telling him, "I'll be the best janitor this hospital has ever had. Otherwise, I'll be sent back to prison."

He laughed and said, "Yeah, that's quite a motivator to do a great job. I'm glad to have you and I'm proud of the stand you took."

Everybody at the hospital treated me well. If they had different political views, which I am certain some did (Hey, it's Idaho) they never let on.

I made sure the place was gleaming. I also did extra work in the kitchen helping wherever I was needed. A little birdie told me that Vi, who ran the kitchen, held a lot of power and it would be prudent for me to be on her good side. She was a big, strong, quiet woman who knew what she wanted and how it was to be done. She did not make work easy, but within two weeks I had free rein in the kitchen. Turns out she was a sweetheart. This esteemed honor was not granted to any of the nurses, doctors, or other employees, not even Mr. Ackerman himself. They were amazed and impressed. I was pretty impressed myself. The Neun allure was finally working.

My boss, Lloyd, was the plant engineer. He kept everything running smoothly which was no small task. He taught me how to keep the big boilers in the basement in tune, how to maintain the emergency generator and to test it to insure it would start automatically if the power to the hospital ever went out. He showed me how to switch out the big oxygen tanks and lots of other maintenance engineer work needed to keep a hospital running. There was a lot to do.

Our realm was the basement. Few others were allowed down there. It was always nice and quiet.

The best benefit of being an employee of the hospital was that the parent company, the Sun Valley Corp, gave me a free ski pass. The bummer was, I worked days. As the winter began, I arranged with Lloyd and Mr. Ackerman to let me come in at eleven a.m. when it snowed which allowed me to get first tracks whenever the good stuff piled up.

My probation officer showed up unannounced one day. He met with Mr. Ackerman and Lloyd and each spoke very highly of the job I was doing. When he talked with me and learned I bought a house and got to go skiing whenever I wanted, he was pissed. "This is not what probation is supposed to be," He exclaimed. But he let it go. I was making his job easy and he had far bigger fish to watch over. When he left, he said he didn't ever want to see or hear from me. I told him he never would, and he never did.

Lloyd retired and Mr. Ackerman promoted me to the plant engineer position. He knew my qualifications were slim but he trusted me and gave me the job. I rose to the task. It was a sweet end to my life of crime.

LEFTY BOWL IN SUN VALLEY

Chapter 24

Torment

I have lived my entire life with the knowledge I murdered four people. Walkin' Death, Cho Mo, Doyle, and Byron. That knowledge has tormented me for every minute of every day throughout life. I have never known peace of mind.

I have tried every rationalization I could think of. The two I return to are:

1. They were all despicable people who deserved to die and
2. I was just a kid, a young stupid kid.

This reasoning does not ring true.

Nothing works.

I try to forgive myself. I have suffered, but at the end of the day I am alive, they are not. I cannot forgive myself. I will never suffer enough. I was never held responsible for these murders by anyone but myself.

I have made a lot of money. Greed is just an addiction, like alcohol and drugs. Merely another twisted addiction.

Those people I murdered; their faces are with me every day and night, without end.

Byron in his car, trapped, screaming, burning to death. His face is seared into my mind. I killed him. I wanted to kill him. Every cell in my body wanted to kill him. I felt good about it. I saved Lucy. That rationalization has not worked.

Taking a simple prison spoon and sharpening it to fashion a razor-sharp shiv gave me purpose. I knew I was going to slit Walkin' Death's throat. I wanted revenge. A reason to live. That reason drained into the dirt with his blood.

When I cut into a steak, I feel my hand thrusting the knife into Doyle. When I see a beater car, I see Doyle. I see his confused eyes and the blood-soaked interior of his car. I have not eaten meat in fifty years.

Every time I drive, I notice the steep road banks and the embedded rocks. I feel my hoedad smash into Cho Mo's head and see his limp body falling and slamming into each rock outcrop, then land in the ditch, dead.

There is no escape from the visions of my deeds.

At the end of every day, I am still alive, and they are not.

I am seventy-one years old and I wonder how much longer I will be able to tolerate myself. When will I decide I have endured enough and end my suffering?

CHAPTER 25

Epilogue

How do sane, rational people justify murder? They do not.

Murder and its justification are reserved exclusively for the insane.

The insane say, "You do not worship my God. Your death is my God's will."

How do the insane justify killing?

I cannot give you the answer. I have never killed anyone.

"Hey, wait, that's bullshit!" you say, "What about Walkin' Death, Cho Mo, Doyle and Byron?" You murdered all those fuckers in cold blood!"

No, I did not. This was just a story.

Nothing more than a fabricated tale.

Be well,

Tim

About the Author

I haven't killed anybody............................ yet.

    I started out as a ski bum. I became a criminal which led to my ex-con status. I was on the road selling machine tools and industrial supplies for the next twenty years. I made the natural transition into designing and fabricating custom furniture, including a number of conference tables.

    I'm the person least likely to write a book. What's the next one about? Your guess is as good as mine. I'm now in awe of writers who come up ideas one after another, like my brother, Mike Neun. Jerk.

    I've led an interesting, varied life. Fun, heartache, more fun, the usual ups and downs privileged white people endure.

    I'm no standout. I'm just a regular guy. I've squandered parts of my life. I've excelled from time to time.

    I live to laugh. I can be serious but it's just not my style.

Glossary

Includes bonus inappropriate terms, sort
of an homage to "alternate facts"

Ah's
As in "Ah's Doyle" Pronounced Eyz

Allure
A quality I lacked as a teenager

Ambit
Hillbilly exclamation of specific
injury. "Ow, am bit!"

Angst
What a ski bum with a short attention
span trying to learn Adobe InDesign feels

Anafractuous
Anna Fractuous, a character
not found in this book

Apropos
As it should be. A Greek appetizer
favored by Eruditey

Babe Magnet
Not a 1964 shit brown Chevy Biscayne
station wagon

Bat Guano
Rain soaked snow. Ideal if the top 2" is partially
frozen

Belay
Involves some rope & knots. Possible
life saving activity

Bivy
A place to spent the night on
a mountain not sleeping

Black hole
Trunk of a 1959 Caddy. Collapsed star
See Schwarzschild radius

Boatload of Shit
Something to shake a stick at

Bombshell
Hot chick

Bozo
A dead clown. Bonehead, Dipshit, trump sup-
porter, Bully

Bridgeport mill
Heavy chunk of iron

Bowline Knot
The rabbit goes around the tree, comes up
through the hole etc. Any knot you come up
with, few will know. Even fewer care.

Ignorant asshole
45th president of the United States

Calculus
Something to do with math

Ceramics
Clay stuff. You'll wear an apron.

Clear weather
No clue, I live in Oregon

Clueless
Normal male lifestyle

Communists
Commie pinko rat bastards. Idealistic. Sounds
good but hasn't worked out yet.

Composure
A behavior many do not display
at the appropriate time.

Concentration
Oh look! Butterflies and unicorns!

Corvair
Death on wheels

Counselor
Another professional to ignore

Coup de Ville
A French term.
Translated: I'm better than you.

Crack
The crack of dawn. The buttcrack of dawn.

Crap
Zeke's old wheelchair, Poop.
1965 Chevy Biscayne station
wagon painted shit brown.

Crips
An unruly gang of kids in wheelchairs.
See Tard

Crevasse
A dangerous gash on a glacier.
A thing to not fall into.

Crud
See Bat Guano

Deer in the headlights
Clueless. You are screwed
& don't yet know it.

Design Element
An object temporarily skewered
by a sharp caddy tail fin, gas
pump, building, pedestrian etc.

Dirty
See filthy

Dork
Dweeb

Dumbfounded
Normal male state of mind.

Dweeb
Dork

Entwined
Twine that has been 'ented.

Erudite
Mythological Greek Goddess

Evaporated
Thick milk, my allure

Festooned
A cartoon with a boatload of fests.

Filthy
See dirty

Flipped the Bird
You actually had to look this up?

Friendship
State of those who buy my book.

Fuckfuckfuck
Lost for words.

Fuckin' A
Self-explanatory. If unsure see Loser.

Gaper
A lousy skier. See Hacker

Glands
Breasts, tits, boobs, mams, Naboth's, Parotid,
Littre. Nut in stuffing box.

GREP
Some typology term. Missed that chapter.

Tim Neun

Grisly
The inside of Doyle's car.

Grounded
See heirloom

Gush
What perspiration and blood does.

Gutter
The things on the edge of my
roof used to collect leaves.

Hacker
Skier with no form, style, grace or
rhythm. Most golfers. See Gaper

Heirloom
A thing, when broken,
grounds you for a week.

Hide & Seek
If you don't know this you had
a shitty childhood.

Hoedad
A tree planting tool. Weapon.
See Hoemoma

                    ʌ
Hoemama
Feminine Hoedad

Hog Heaven
Bat Guano conditions in Sun Valley

Hosed
Screwed

Hydraulic
Thick star formation region in the
Coma cluster. Ulics of Hydras

Hydros
Greek for thick. Thick headed.

Idaho
Potatoes, rednecks, white supremacists, guns,
more potatoes, Sun Valley

Kerning
To kern

Lacrosse
A French cross

Lifting weights
Got me.

Logorrhea
Diarrhea of the mouth. To pontificate.

Loser
Those who could care less about my book

Love
Way too many definitions for this,
plus it's not in the book.

Tim Neun

Lugie
Semi solid mass of Phlegm, sputum
& glerck that can be launched long
distances with pinpoint accuracy.

Malaise
The white stuff used on ham sandwiches

Masterpiece
Not what I made in Ceramics class

Mind numbing
English, Math, Social Studies,etc.
Editing a book.

Mt. Vesuvius
Adolescent acne, bummer for
those living in Pompeii

Mulct
A river in northern California

Neutrinos
Little massless doodads. Billions
pass through every square inch
of your body every second.

Newbie
An unprepared person, thrust into a new
situation. Commonly prefaced with fuckin'.

No Sweat
Perspiration-less. Easy. See Piece of Cake.

Ominous
You are fucked, you just don't quite know it.

Orphans
Words or single lines of text at the bottom of a column or pages that become separated from the other lines in the paragraph. Typological equivalent to a gaper.

PCT
Pacific Crest Trail.
Pretty Cohesive Turnstile.

Penetrate
What I did not do as a teenager

Piss ant
See loser and newbie

Planet like mass
1959 Caddy

Potters wheel
A spinny thing that clay flies off of.

Profound
Orphic (helpful 'eh)

Protuberance
1959 Caddy tail fins.
Tissue stuffed glands

Pummel
To beat up. Horrendous ceramic clay figurines. A thing gymnasts use.

Rain
All I know. I live in Oregon.

Tim Neun

Reprimanded
Ego deflation technique

Scratch
Money. A minor abrasion. An injury
that taxes Dr. Midnite's medical prowess.

Screwing
See thrust washer

Sequencer
A metal/plastic/wood/paper thing that
sequences things/words/feelings.

Shank
An embarrassing mis-hit in golf.
See Hacker

Shiv
A crude prison knife. See Shank

Slope
The term non skiers use instead of mountain.
"Let's go schussing on the slopes!"

Socrates
Some old wise dead dude

Sputum
Lugie, Phlegum. Semi solid mass of glerck that
can be launched long distances with
pinpoint accuracy.

Sub-par
Authors level of writing achievement.

Supple
Perhaps a quality Yoga people have.

Sussed
Dissed

Tard
Slang for retard. If used, defines the utterer as an unenlightened shit for brains.

Taro root
Mashed up stuff not eaten in Grosse Ille

Telestic
Telescoping ski pole

Tits
Tissue paper stuffed protuberance. See glands

TLTLU
Too Lazy To Look Up

Unvarnished
Without varnish

Upset
Feminine equivalent of being pissed off

Vented
Invented

Whitey
Honky

Woody
Boner. Hard on etc. ad nauseam.
50s & 60s cars with plastic looking wood plastered on them.

WooWoo
Derogatory but accurate term for overly sincere spirituality

Discussion Guide

*E*ar to Ear glanced off the surface of a few serious moral issues. Murder, war, the demise of the gas cap accessed by a push button on the taillight.

I've posed a few questions here for you discuss quietly amongst yourselves. My hope being, through speaking respectfully and gently, listening to what others say and feel, you will gain empathy and an understanding of each others opinions. It is an honor for me to provide this service to you, my sophisticated and valued reader.

1. How would you deal with your inner self after murdering some worthless dickhead?

2. The people Tim murdered were the penultimate lowlifes. Does that justify his love of skiing?

3. Would you murder some swine who threatened to kill you? Would you be able to recite, verbatim, the stand your ground laws of Arkansas? If so, my real name is Mike Neun and I live in Changmai, Thailand.

4. Refusing induction into the armed forces while others served and died. How do you feel about that?

5. Was the 1964 Mustang fastback truly an abominable snow car? [1]

6. Why did the push button access taillight gas cap design not flourish?

7. Should juveniles who murder bullies be sentenced as adults?

8. Should juveniles who murder bullies, that deserved it, be congratulated?

9. The Vietnam war. Did you trust what our lying asshole leaders were telling us?

10. Why did Byron hassle Joan? Did he secretly have a crush on her? Was she secretly smitten by him? Why does anybody fall for bozos like Byron?

11. Is it OK to just wing the facts about actual places like the glaciers on the North and Middle Sisters?

12. Sea Lion Caves. Is it worth the money? Have you ever smelled anything so foul as a million pounds of sea lion shit? If so, where?

13. Is lazy research justified in fiction?

14. Is just making shit up about real places OK?

15. Can there ever be too much cursing?

16. Is it OK to bring a razor sharp, nine inch shiv to a discussion guide meeting? Are masks required?

17. Can murder be humorous?

18. Should murder be humorous?

19. Is humorous murder distasteful?

20. Was leaving the solo and going to the store to buy junk food in the spirit of Outward Bound?

21. Was having to drink pine needle tea a valid reason to go buy hot dogs and kill Doyle?

22. Should the gas mileage of the 1959 Cadillac Coup De Ville have been a concern to the owner in 1962 when gas was twenty-three cents per gallon?[2]

23. Is peaking on LSD, while trapped in a claustrophobic elevator filled with the stink of a billion pounds of sea lion shit along with a bunch of straight people, reasons enough, to freak out?

24. Is it wise to take LSD with an unstable person?

25. Does LSD make a stable person, unstable?

26. How does a meteor, traveling from the far side of the Milky Way Galaxy nearly attain the speed of light? Would the A that permeates the galaxy slow it down or speed it up?[3]

27. Was Minion Pro a suitable font to use in this book?

28. Is stashing extra matches in your shirt collar acceptable behavior knowing you are going to be stuck in a rain forest for the next four days?

29. Should a fictional novel contain images?

30. Is leading a bunch of newbies on a hike, around in circles in order to exhaust them, acceptable?

31. If stealing Indian lands works for you, would you also accept naming all the natural sites after white people? If so, please tell us why because everybody wants to hear what will be, your stupid fucking answer.

32. Is grinding up pumice making it look like cocaine then selling it to some bully commendable?

33. Would giving it to the bully, without charging them, be even funnier?

When Blazing Away

A. Give them more LSD, maybe some whiskey and a bunch of really strong weed.

B. Stay with them and talk them though it using gentle words of support for the next ten fucking hours?

C. Stay with them for the next ten(6)fucking hours knowing you will both end up stark raving mad.

D. Is telling them you are a flesh eating alien while flapping your arms erratically and making scary alien faces while speaking in some alien language you just made up, just to see what happens, cruel or an experience they will cherish for the rest of their life?

E. Scream at them, "You have to drive to the coast (don't tell them which one) by yourself to escape the aliens, RIGHT NOW!!!? Could a mean spirited but hilarious prank result in a life long friendship?

F. Run like the wind and let them sort it out by themselves?

G. Make them listen to "Stayin' Alive" by the BeeGees with headphones on ('cause you don't want to ever hear that fucking song ever again) for six hours nonstop. Make sure it's really loud.

ENDNOTES

Questions 5, 22 and 26 were bonus trick questions. Here are the answers:

1 The Mustang fastback wasn't produced until
    1965
2 The Coup De Ville was not offered in 1959
3 Averaged out, how many atoms of Aether are
    in each cubic meter of empty space?
    A. Zero
    B. 1.37627
    C. 43.376273
    D. 43.3762731